Santa Paws
on
Christmas Island

Merry Christmas

Mrs. Bardo

2006

Read all the Santa Paws adventures:

SANTA PAWS

*SANTA PAWS, THE RETURN OF
SANTA PAWS*

SANTA PAWS, COME HOME

SANTA PAWS TO THE RESCUE

SANTA PAWS, OUR HERO

SANTA PAWS AND THE NEW PUPPY

SANTA PAWS SAVES THE DAY

*SANTA PAWS AND THE CHRISTMAS
STORM*

Santa Paws
ON
Christmas Island

by Kris Edwards

AN
APPLE
PAPERBACK

SCHOLASTIC INC.

New York   Toronto   London   Auckland   Sydney
Mexico City   New Delhi   Hong Kong   Buenos Aires

ISBN 13: 978-0-439-88812-7
ISBN 10: 0-439-88812-3

Cover illustration by Robert Hunt
Cover design by Timothy Hall

12 11 10 9 8 7 6 5 4 3 2 1   6 7 8 9 10 11/0

Printed in the U.S.A.   40

First printing, November 2006

For Gail and Virginia

Santa Paws

on

Christmas Island

1

"Snow day!"

Gregory Callahan thought those must be the two most beautiful words in the English language. What could be better than waking up to that certain special muffled quiet, where the only sound was the occasional rumble of a snowplow making its way down the street?

Gregory knew there would be no school that day even before he opened his eyes. On the weather channel the night before, they'd talked about a big storm coming. But so many times these storms never really showed up. Heavy, deep snow would fall to the north or to the south, but somehow Oceanport, Rhode Island always missed out. Oh, maybe they'd get a dusting, or even an inch or two. But what good was that? You couldn't snowboard or go sledding or build a snowman with a couple of inches of snow. Gregory could hardly believe it was almost Christmas. Where was the snow?

This morning was different. When his clock radio clicked on, the first thing Gregory heard was the voice of Uncle Andy, the morning DJ on The Zone, Gregory's favorite station. "Yo, cats and kittens!" Uncle Andy was saying, in his hyped-up morning voice. "Check it out! This whole *state* is on vacation! That's right, kiddies, just about every school in Rhode Island is locking its doors today. State offices, too. If you don't *have* to go anywhere, stay put. That's what the state troopers are saying, and that's what Uncle Andy says, too. The roads are a *mess*, with over two feet of snow along the coast."

"Yesss!" Gregory leapt out of bed, throwing a fist into the air. He did a quick victory dance in his plaid flannel pajamas, waving his hands as he turned around in a circle. "Come on, Santa Paws!" he called to his dog. "Snow day! Rise and shine!"

Santa Paws, who had been sleeping peacefully at the foot of Gregory's bed, opened one eye. Wasn't it a little early for this kind of thing? He let out a huge yawn, hoping Gregory would understand that what he *really* wanted was to go back to sleep and finish the excellent dream he had been having about romping through a whole field of Milk-Bone bushes.

"Come on, big guy!" Gregory said. "Dance with me!"

The dog rose slowly to his feet and hopped off the bed with a groan. He wasn't a puppy anymore! Sometimes he was stiff in the morning. But if Gregory wanted to dance, the dog was happy to do it. Lots of times, after they "danced," Gregory would give Santa Paws some sort of treat. Usually it was a Milk-Bone, which was always great. But since it was just about breakfast time anyway, Santa Paws might get something special mixed in with his kibble. Maybe it would be cottage cheese or leftover spaghetti, or even—best of all!—some of Evelyn and Abigail's canned cat food. Evelyn always hissed and made a fuss when she caught Santa Paws eating her food, but what was she going to do about it? An old tiger cat was no match at all for a strapping German shepherd mix like him. And as for the younger Abigail, the Callahan's black cat, she was feisty, but she adored Santa Paws. He was her hero, and he was welcome to help himself to her food anytime.

Santa Paws was a hero to lots of people and animals. He had a way of sensing danger or trouble. If someone was hurt, or scared, or needed any kind of help, Santa Paws was there. He had become famous for his rescues, many of which seemed to take place around Christmas time. That's how he had gotten his name.

Santa Paws would help anyone who needed him. But the most important people in his life were the Callahans, the family that had taken him in when he was just a tiny stray puppy, alone on the streets. He would do *anything* for them. And if that meant dancing, so be it.

3

He jumped up and put his paws on Gregory's shoulders. Santa Paws was a big dog—he weighed in at around ninety pounds at the vet's office—but he was light as a feather leaning against Gregory. They waltzed around the room a few times. "Snow day, snow day!" Gregory sang. "Woo-hoo! Yeah! Ooh, baby!"

Then Santa Paws dropped back onto all fours, and Gregory jumped up onto his bed. He started playing air guitar, throwing his head back and strumming a power chord.

"Great sound, bro!"

Gregory froze in place. A blush crept up his cheeks as he snuck a peek toward the door. There she was: his older sister, Patricia. She was standing with her arms folded across her chest, leaning against the door frame with a superior smirk on her face. She was looking as chic as always in purple and black pajamas printed with teddy bears wearing sunglasses. "Get down! Play that funky music!" she cried.

Gregory *did* get down—off his bed. "Go ahead, make fun of me," he said, still blushing. "Who cares? It's a snow day!" He waved a hand toward his window, at all the snow. "Let's get out there!"

Patricia nodded. "I'm with you," she said. "I already called Aunt Emily to asked if Lucy and Miranda and Cookie would like to come sledding with us. Uncle Steve is going to bring them over so we can all eat breakfast together."

"Excellent," said Gregory. He really loved his two young cousins. Even though there was quite an age difference—Patricia and Gregory were seventeen and sixteen and Miranda and Lucy were six and three—all four cousins were best friends.

And Cookie, their dog, was best friends with Santa Paws. In fact, Santa Paws had been the one to bring the energetic, little curly-haired black puppy home with him. She was a stray, just as he had been, and he knew the Callahans would make room for her in their lives. As it turned out, Cookie bonded so strongly with Miranda that it soon became obvious that they belonged together. Now Cookie lived with Miranda and Lucy and their parents, Steve and Emily. Steve Callahan was a policeman on the Oceanport force, and Emily was a busy advertising executive who commuted to the city a few days a week.

"Maybe today's the day for Miranda's first snowboard lesson," Gregory said. He knew that his young cousin looked up to him. In fact, she probably thought he was sort of like a rock star, or a famous athlete, or some other celebrity. He was into snowboarding, so Miranda had decided she wanted to do it, too. He would be generous and patient with her and teach her everything he knew. That was just the kind of guy he was. Why couldn't Tonya Sweetser understand that? Tonya-the-gorgeous was Gregory's lab partner in biology.

They took turns looking through a microscope every Tuesday and Thursday afternoon—but she still barely seemed to notice that he was alive. Gregory wondered if Tonya would like him better if he put gel in his hair and spiked it up. He checked the mirror. Nah, he just wasn't the gel type. He'd have to think of something else.

"Greg? Earth to Greg?" Patricia was snapping her fingers in front of his face. "Wake up, buddy. Let's get dressed and get out in that beautiful snow. We're burning daylight!"

Burning daylight? Where did Patricia *get* these sayings? Gregory gave her a puzzled look.

"Just—hurry up, that's all," Patricia said. "We haven't had a good snowstorm in years. I want to enjoy this one to the max."

Downstairs, the mood was very different. Eileen Callahan sighed as she stared out the kitchen window. "I can't believe it's only December and I'm already tired of winter!" she said. "I look out at all that snow and all I can think about is what a pain it's going to be to shovel it, and how I'll probably slip on the front walk, and what if the power goes out, and . . ." She took a sip of coffee and sighed again.

"I would think you'd be glad to have a snow day," her husband said. He was sitting at the kitchen table, polishing off a bowl of oatmeal. Evelyn, the tiger cat, sat purring on his lap, occasionally batting a paw at Abigail, the black cat,

6

who was sitting on the floor next to Mr. Callahan's chair.

Abigail, too, liked Tom Callahan's lap. Sometimes—often!—he spilled a bit of food while he was eating. But there was no way Evelyn was going to share the man's lap. For now, Abigail would have to content herself with lurking on the floor near Mr. Callahan's fluffy bunny slippers, hoping that some food would make it all the way to the floor.

Mr. Callahan was a writer. He worked at home, with lots and lots of breaks for coffee, tea, the newspaper, e-mail, or anything else that was distracting and enjoyable. It didn't much matter to him whether it snowed or rained or hailed, especially since he had long ago sworn off snow shoveling. "Bad back," he always pleaded, putting a hand to his lower back. His back never actually hurt, but he'd heard that snow shoveling could *make* it hurt.

Mrs. Callahan was a teacher at the same high school Gregory and Patricia attended. She put in long days and often brought home a briefcase full of papers to correct. "Well, yes, I can catch up on some work," she said to her husband now. "But first I've got to shovel. It's just a huge bother."

As she looked out the window, a police cruiser pulled up. "Steve's here," she said. "And it looks as if he's brought Miranda and Lucy and Cookie, too."

"I'd better put on more oatmeal," said Mr. Callahan. Gently, he tried to push Evelyn off his lap. She wasn't budging. "Come on, Evelyn," he said. "We have company." Finally, he pushed his chair back and put the cat down. Evelyn gave a meow in protest as she was unceremoniously plopped onto the floor. She took a moment to shoot a dirty look at Mr. Callahan before she stalked out of the kitchen, tail held high. Who did he think he was, disturbing *her*? She should be the one to decide when it was time to move.

Eileen Callahan watched through the window as her brother-in-law floundered toward the house through the drifts. He was carrying Lucy and holding Miranda's hand. Cookie dove through the snow, ears and tail up. She always looked happy. Cookie had lots and lots of energy.

Both girls were dressed in snowsuits, boots, hats, mittens, and scarves. "Oh, boy, do I remember dressing little kids to play outside," said Eileen. "It seemed to take hours to get them into all their gear. Then they'd have to go to the bathroom, and it would all have to come off. When they finally got outside, they'd play for about three minutes before they wanted to come back in for hot chocolate."

"Hot chocolate!" said Tom. "Great idea! I'll get some going."

By the time Steve made it to the door, his police uniform was covered in snow. He stomped off in the entryway while Mrs. Callahan wiped off Cookie's paws and helped the girls out of their snowsuits. As soon as they were stripped down to their long underwear, Miranda and Lucy raced upstairs to find their cousins and Santa Paws, with Cookie scrambling after them.

"You look tired, Steve," said Eileen, as she led him into the kitchen.

He nodded. "Double shift," he said. "I was out all night, helping folks who slid off the road or lost their power. I went home to shower and shave and change clothes, but now I'm headed out again for another few hours."

"Oh, dear," said Eileen.

"Emily's exhausted, too," Steve said. "She had a big presentation due at work today, and she was up half the night finishing it. Now, of course, she can't get there with the roads such a mess. She just wants to sleep in today. That's why she was thrilled when Patricia offered to take the girls sledding." He sighed. "I never thought I'd say it, but I'm already sick of winter."

"That's exactly what I said!" Eileen stared at him. "I mean, why do we put up with it? If we were smart, we'd live in South Carolina, or New Mexico, or somewhere with *normal* weather."

Steve nodded. "You know, in my whole life I've never once gone on vacation to a warm place in winter," he said. "Everybody else goes to the Bahamas or the Caribbean. Where do we go? Maine.

Vermont. New Hampshire . . . states that are even colder than our own!"

"That's just what I was thinking when I woke up this morning." Mrs. Callahan poured Steve a cup of coffee while her husband fixed him a bowl of oatmeal with brown sugar and cream. "Why hasn't this family ever celebrated Christmas in, say, Florida?"

"I'll tell you why," Mr. Callahan said. "Because we can't take the pets. Remember? We've looked into this before." He held up a hand and ticked off fingers. "Cruise ships don't take pets. It takes nearly twenty-four hours to drive to Florida, which is crazy. Dogs and cats can't travel on the train. And if they go on a plane, they have to go in the cargo hold, where it's cold and dark and scary. Unless you can afford to charter your own private jet, which—do I really need to point this out?—we can't."

"True," said Mrs. Callahan. "And it just wouldn't be Christmas without the pets. I could never leave them at home or, heaven forbid, put them in a kennel. I'm sure you and Emily feel the same way, right, Steve?"

Steve didn't seem to hear her.

"Steve?" she asked.

"I'm just thinking," he said slowly. "Have I ever told you about Big Jim Jessup and the favor he owes me?"

Just then the adults were interrupted by the

clatter of four kids and two dogs thumping down the stairs and running into the kitchen. The next half hour was a whirlwind of activity as everyone ate breakfast and then climbed into their outdoor clothes. Gregory had a brief moment of panic when he couldn't find his snowboard, but his mom was able to unearth it in the garage, where it was tucked behind the summer patio furniture.

It was a glorious day. Gregory could not have been happier as he stood at the top of Bailey's Hill, his snowboard under one arm. Winter was the *best*! There must have been fifty kids out there already, and everybody was having a ball. They slid down the hill on sleds, toboggans, skis, snow-boards, tubes, cafeteria trays, and even pieces of cardboard. The white hillside was dotted with the bright colors of their jackets and hats, and the air rang with their laughter and shrieks.

Gregory and his cousins played on the hill for hours. Gregory sought out the steepest runs and flew down them with Santa Paws galloping at his heels. Patiently, he showed Miranda how to ride her junior snowboard on the gentler part of the hill. He joined Patricia and Lucy on a top-speed sled ride that ended with all three of them rolling around in the snow, laughing hysterically, with Cookie licking their faces.

Everybody was having the time of their lives.

And then . . .

Santa Paws and Gregory were at the top of the hill when it happened. The dog knew there was something wrong before Gregory even heard the screams. Santa Paws stood very, very still for a moment, his nose quivering in the air and his ears on alert. Then the dog took off like a brown bullet, tearing down the hill to see how he could help.

2

By the time Gregory made it down the hill, a crowd of about fifteen kids had gathered. "What happened?" Gregory asked, as he stepped out of his snowboard bindings.

"It's my sister. She went over that jump on her sled," said a boy in a blue hat with yellow stars. His lower lip was trembling and his face was pale. "Now she can't get up."

Gregory pushed his way through the crowd. Santa Paws was standing over a small girl in a pink snowsuit who lay curled in the snow, crying. There was a spreading blotch of red beneath her leg. Gregory felt his heart thump. This did not look good. He felt in his pocket for his cell phone. Maybe he should call 911! But the phone wasn't there. He must have left it at home.

Just then, Santa Paws looked up at him. Gregory nodded. "We need help, big guy," he said.

The dog knew exactly what that meant. "Help" was in the big building where the people in uniforms worked. They had a white truck that had special spinning lights. The truck sang while it raced along, a loud wailing noise that would make any dog want to howl.

"Hold on a second, Santa Paws," Gregory said. Quickly, he unhooked the zipper pull from his jacket. It was in the shape of a snowboard. Maybe it would help the EMTs understand where the trouble was. He attached it to his dog's collar. "OK, buddy," he said, giving Santa Paws a scratch between the ears. "Go get help!"

The dog took a moment to get his bearings. The building was—that way! He gathered all his energy and took off, running as fast as he could. Snow sprayed up behind him, and he heard the shouts of the children. "Yay, Santa Paws!" "Bring help, Santa Paws!"

"What's going on?" Patricia asked. She and Lucy and Miranda had just joined the group on the hill. Cookie pranced along with them. Her black fur was so thoroughly covered in snow that she looked more like a white dog.

"Accident," Gregory said shortly. "Santa Paws went to the hospital for help."

The little black dog trotted over to the girl. When Cookie nuzzled her cheek, the girl opened her eyes. Her sobs slowed as she looked up at the friendly, furry face above her own.

"Are you OK?" Patricia knelt to talk to the girl. "What's your name?"

The girl started sobbing again. Gently, Cookie lay down beside her. Cookie always knew how to comfort hurt people. "I'm Sarah. My—my leg hurts," the girl finally managed to say. She reached out a small, pink-mittened hand to touch Cookie.

"I bet it does," Patricia said. "I'm Patricia. May I check it out?" With her uncle Steve's urging, Patricia had taken a first aid class that fall. Patricia had often thought she might like to be a police officer someday. She liked knowing more about how to help people. Gently, she touched the girl's leg, moving her hands up and down to feel for broken bones. She didn't feel any of the swelling or "deformity"—a weird bump or a strange angle—she had been taught to look for, but she noticed a rip near the bottom right leg of the girl's snowsuit. "May I unzip the ankle of your snow pants?" she asked. She knew the next step was to expose the injury, if possible, and make sure the bleeding was stopped.

When the girl nodded, Patricia carefully pulled up the zipper on the girl's puffy pink pants. Inside, the ankle of her pink-and-white striped long underwear was stained red. "Did you hit your ankle on the sled runner, maybe?" Patricia asked, as she rolled up the long underwear.

"I—I think maybe so," Sarah said, gasping in pain. "It hurts!"

"I can see why," Patricia said, looking down

at Sarah's ankle. It was very white, with a gash of red running across it. "You do have a nasty laceration there."

"A what?" Sarah looked frightened.

"That just means a cut," Patricia explained quickly. "But I can see that it's already stopped bleeding, so I don't think you'll need stitches."

After she had checked the ankle, Patricia made sure that Sarah wasn't hurt anywhere else, and asked her some questions about whether she had hit her head or hurt her neck. Then she made sure Sarah was as comfortable and warm as possible while they waited for help to arrive.

While Patricia was helping the little girl, Santa Paws was doing his part. When he left the hill, he ran as fast as he could. He watched carefully for cars but kept to the road whenever possible, to avoid the huge snow drifts on either side. Salt that had been spread on the road to melt the snow stung his feet, but the pain didn't bother him. Nothing bothered Santa Paws when he was on the job.

He ran and ran, sliding now and then but always catching himself before he fell. Once a car slowed down and somebody yelled, "Santa Paws! Where are you going? Do you need a ride?" But he was too focused on getting to the helping place to pay attention.

Finally, Santa Paws found himself at the door of the big building where the white trucks lived. He whined and scratched and barked until someone opened the door. It was a woman in a blue jumpsuit. "Hey, look who's here!" she said. "You know what that means. Somebody needs our help." She pushed a button and an alarm sounded, bringing several other people to the door. They were wearing jumpsuits, too.

Santa Paws barked and backed away, taking a few steps in the direction he'd come from, to show them the way.

"OK, boy, OK!" said the woman. "We know you'll show us where to go. Someone is getting the ambulance now." She peered more closely at the dog. "What's that on your collar?" she asked, when she saw the shiny tag. She bent to check it out. "Hmm," she said. "A snowboard. I wonder if that's a clue."

"The only hill around here that's big enough for snowboarding is Bailey's," said the man behind her.

Santa Paws barked. That was the same word he had heard Gregory use that morning! He recognized the sound.

"That must be it," said the man.

The big garage doors opened and the dog saw one of those big white trucks pull out. It stopped and a door opened. "Hop in, pal," said the driver. Santa Paws got in, along with the woman, who had put a parka over her jump suit. He sat on the front seat, nose forward and every muscle quivering in excitement. In a moment, he knew, the driver would push a button and the truck would howl like a wolf. That meant they were on the way. That meant the little girl would get help soon.

Back at the hill, the sound of a siren reached Gregory's ears. "The ambulance is here!" shouted a boy at the edge of the crowd. Everybody watched as the emergency vehicle pulled up at the bottom of the hill. "Good boy," Gregory said, under his breath when he saw Santa Paws leap out. "Good boy."

Patricia stroked Sarah's hair. "They'll take good care of you," she told the frightened girl. "Don't be scared. They'll call your mom, too. By the time you get to the hospital, I bet she'll be waiting there for you."

The EMTs ran up the hill, led by Santa Paws. His head was high and his tail waved proudly. This was what he did best! It always made him feel so happy to help people. When they reached Sarah, Santa Paws barked twice to signal that they had arrived at the right place. Then he went over to Gregory.

"Good boy, Santa Paws!" said Gregory, ruffling his dog's ears.

Santa Paws leaned contentedly into Gregory's leg. He knew there would be special treats coming his way when they got home. But he would help no matter what. He didn't need Milk-Bones for a reward. Not that he would ever turn one down. . . .

The two EMTs knelt near Sarah. "I think she'll be OK," Patricia reported. "I'm Patricia, and this is Sarah, a nine-year-old female who has sustained a minor laceration. Vital signs are normal: pulse is eighty-two, respirations are about fourteen a minute. Pupils are equal and reactive, no report of loss of consciousness, no sign of any significant injury other than to the ankle."

Gregory thought he saw one of the EMTs shoot a smile at the other. But they both nodded seriously. "Good job," said the woman. She checked Sarah out some more, then wrapped a bandage around the cut. "I think Patricia is right that your injury isn't serious," she said to Sarah, "but why don't we take you for a ride to the hospital and make sure?"

While the woman was talking to Sarah, the other EMT talked to her brother and got their home number. He pulled out a cell phone and stood aside to make a quick call. Snapping shut the phone, he reported, "Your mom will meet us at the emergency room, Sarah. Now, can you stand up with our help? Don't put any weight on that leg. We'll make a chair out of our arms and carry you down the hill."

A few minutes later, Patricia, Gregory, Lucy, and Miranda watched from the top of the hill as the ambulance drove away.

"I don't want to snowboard anymore," Miranda said, grabbing Gregory's hand. "Can we go home now?"

"Sure," said Gregory. "I'm pretty tired, anyway. And these dogs both deserve a big treat."

Steve's police cruiser was back out in front of Tom Callahan's house when the cousins returned home. "I wonder if he heard about what happened on his scanner," Patricia said.

Sure enough, Steve knew all the details of the rescue, from Santa Paws' quick action to Patricia's excellent first-aid work. "Nicely done," he said to his niece, giving her a high five when she walked into the kitchen.

"It was nothing," said Patricia. But Gregory saw her pleased smile.

"Santa Paws and Cookie helped a lot!" Miranda reported.

"I bet they did," said Mr. Callahan. "Let's see, what do we have for a couple of good dogs?" He opened a cupboard and pulled out a box of Milk-Bones. "These will do for Santa Paws," he said, passing the box to Gregory. "But what about Cookie?"

Cookie did not eat dog treats. She turned up her nose at Milk-Bones, holding out for *real* cookies, *people* cookies. Her favorites were homemade peanut butter or oatmeal raisin, but she would put up with vanilla wafers if that was all there was.

"I think we have some pecan sandies," said Mrs. Callahan.

Cookie's ears went up when she heard that. She loved those cookies, too! Right away she sat up prettily with her paws held high, the way Patricia had taught her. She watched alertly as Mrs. Callahan opened the package. Why was everybody laughing?

"Here you go, sweetie," said Eileen, giving the black dog a cookie. Gregory gave Santa Paws *two* Milk-Bones. The big guy deserved that—and more.

"So, should we tell them the big news?" Steve asked Mr. and Mrs. Callahan. Gregory noticed his uncle was looking a lot less tired than he had that morning. In fact, his eyes were sparkling.

"What's up?" Gregory asked. He noticed that his mother looked pretty happy, too.

"Well, as soon as I could get off duty, I started making some phone calls," said Steve. "You may have heard your mother and me grumbling about winter weather this morning. I decided it was time to do something about it."

Gregory looked suspicious. "What do you mean?" he asked. "We kids happen to like winter, you know." He and Patricia exchanged a look. Their parents had a way of making decisions for them when it came to Christmas vacation. Last year, they'd dragged the whole family to a tiny island way off the coast of Maine. The year before

21

that, it had been a skiing vacation in Vermont. Maybe it was true that Gregory and Patricia had ended up having a fabulous time in *both* places, but that still didn't mean it was fair for their parents to make such big decisions without consulting them. Maybe you could get away with that kind of thing around kids Miranda and Lucy's age. But Gregory and Patricia were practically *adults* for Pete's sake. Patricia would be able to *vote* next year!

"So, what's the big news?" Patricia asked warily.

"Well, it's time to pack your bags," Steve said with a big smile. "And don't forget your sunglasses and bathing suits. We're going to Florida!"

3

The captain's voice came over the loudspeakers. "We've reached cruising altitude, folks. You're welcome to walk around the cabin now, or just sit back and enjoy the trip!"

Patricia leaned back in her seat, sinking happily into the soft, brown leather. She could hardly believe that she and her entire family were on their way to celebrate Christmas in Florida. Everything had happened so fast since that memorable snow day a week ago!

She and Gregory had, naturally, been outraged when their uncle announced that they were going to Florida. Where was the fairness? Didn't the kids get *any* voice in big decisions—like where to spend Christmas?

Mom, Dad, and Steve had just sat there in the kitchen, nodding and smiling as Patricia and Gregory vented. Santa Paws and Cookie hid under the table. The dogs just *hated* it when people yelled.

And Evelyn and Abigail fled to their favorite hiding places: in the linen closet and under the bed in Patricia's room, respectively. Lucy crawled onto her father's lap, and Miranda stood by Patricia's chair looking as if she were about to burst into tears.

"... and you can't drag me along if I don't want to go," Patricia finished her tirade, arms folded across her chest. "I'm over sixteen and I can do what I want. I'll stay here with Rachel, or some other friend."

"Yeah," Gregory said. "I mean, me, too. I'm happy staying right here in Oceanport. What's so great about Florida?"

"Two words," said Steve, grinning. "Sun and surf."

Patricia and Gregory were momentarily speechless. Steve had a point. Why were they resisting? They both loved the beach. And they both loved sunshine just as much as they loved snow. How bad could Florida be?

"Still," said Patricia, after a moment. "Obviously the pets wouldn't be able to come. So what kind of family vacation is that? I'm not going anywhere without Santa Paws and Cookie."

Under the table, the dogs heard their names. They thumped their tails in unison. Maybe they were about to get more treats!

"We wouldn't *think* of planning a vacation without the pets," Mom said indignantly.

"That's the beauty of this plan," Steve said. And

then he explained everything. "You guys know who Big Jim Jessup is, right?" he began.

"Of course," said Gregory.

"Duh," said Patricia. "It's not like we live under a rock, just because Mom and Dad limit our TV viewing."

Everybody knew who Big Jim was. You couldn't miss him if you tried. He was a Texas millionaire—no, make that *zillionaire*—and everything he did made the front page, or at least the gossip columns. He was probably the richest guy in the USA. And he really was big. Like, seven feet tall. Plus, he always wore a giant white cowboy hat. Big Jim owned a chain of stores called—what else?—Big Jim's. He also owned yachts, race horses, a basketball team, a couple of ski resorts, and even, Patricia had once read in *People* magazine, a small town in Alabama.

And he owned airplanes—private jets that whisked him and his current beautiful wife (Patricia thought he was on marriage number five) wherever they wanted to go. Each airplane was purple—Big Jim's favorite color—with a big white cowboy hat painted on its tail. Patricia approved of his color choice: Purple was *her* favorite color, too.

"Well," Steve went on with his explanation, "what you may not know is that I once met Big Jim."

"Come on, Steve," Tom Callahan urged his

brother. "Don't be modest. There's more to the story than that." He turned to Patricia and Gregory. "Your uncle saved Big Jim's life."

"What?" Patricia asked. Her mouth hung open in surprise. "When?"

Steve waved a hand. "It was nothing, really. It was back before I was a police officer. I was working as a security guard at this big office building in Boston. A building Big Jim owned. Basically my job was to stand around outside the building and look serious. Anyway, Big Jim was there one day for a meeting. When he left he was so busy talking on his cell phone that he stepped into the street, right into the path of a bus!"

"Whoa!" said Gregory. "What did you do?"

"What would anybody do?" Steve asked with a shrug. "I grabbed the guy and pulled him out of the street."

"And saved his life, just as I said!" Dad added.

"Well, maybe," Steve said. "Anyway, all the things you've heard about Big Jim are true: How he likes to tip people with fifty-dollar bills, and how he never forgets anybody who was good to him. That day, he told me he owed me a big favor. He gave me his private phone number and told me to call on him for anything I wanted, anytime. I told him he didn't owe me anything, but he just smiled at me and patted my shoulder with one of his huge hands. 'Son,' he said, in that Texas twang, 'someday you'll take me up on it.'"

Steve smiled. "I guess he was right!"

"You'll never believe it," Mom said. "When Steve called Big Jim today he got put right through as soon as he said who he was. Just like that!" She snapped her fingers. "Amazing."

And that, Patricia thought now as she gazed out the airplane window, was that. One phone call, and the entire Callahan clan was on its way to Christmas Island. The island was just off the coast of Florida, connected by a long bridge. They could hardly believe it when they heard they'd be spending Christmas on Christmas Island! And the Callahans were going first class all the way. Big Jim had arranged it all.

All four adults and four kids, plus two dogs and two cats, would fly down on one of his private jets. They would stay at his newest resort, The Oasis—all expenses paid. And they would fly back home in style. It was like they had fallen into some kind of reality show—and they were the grand prize winners!

Big Jim had asked for just one thing in return when he heard that Mr. Callahan was a writer: He wanted Tom to write a story about the hotel, an article he could put in an advertising brochure. The Oasis was so new that it hadn't caught on yet, and Big Jim wanted to promote it as a first-class family resort.

Patricia and Gregory had stopped fighting the

Christmas-in-Florida idea as soon as they'd heard the details. This was going to be the vacation of a lifetime, no question about it.

They'd barely had time to digest the news before the big day had arrived. At nine o'clock on a bright, shiny December morning, everyone was gathered at the Callahan's house, ready to go.

Patricia had agonized over her outfit: What does one wear on a private jet? She had finally decided on low-slung jeans paired with the purple mohair sweater set she'd begged for last Christmas, along with her new black boots and a casual-yet-hip purse she'd bought for herself the week before while she was doing her Christmas shopping.

She had looked around at her family and noted that, as usual, nobody else seemed concerned with appearances. Gregory was in jeans and a Team USA sweatshirt. Mom was wearing her usual schoolteacher clothes: a denim jumper and a turtleneck. Steve and Emily and the two younger cousins were dressed in their typical weekend getups of jeans, T-shirts, and sneakers. At least, Patricia noted with relief, Dad had remembered for once to swap his wacky bunny slippers for actual shoes.

The dogs looked snappy: Santa Paws in his red-and-green Christmas collar, and Cookie in a glittery pink leather number Patricia had picked up at a pet store sale. And the cats were traveling in Pet Taxis. The matching carriers had different color bows: a red, white, and green plaid bow for Abigail and a Kelly green bow for Evelyn. All was quiet inside the boxes. The vet had given the cats pills to keep them calm during the flight. They had never flown before, and the Callahans wanted to make it as painless for them—and for the passengers—as possible.

Patricia had gulped when the big black stretch limo pulled up in front of the Callahans' house. Was this for real? She pinched herself, wishing mightily that one of her friends would walk by right now and see *this*.

"Look, it's Santa!" Miranda cried, pointing at the driver. Sure enough, the man climbing out of the driver's seat was wearing a red-and-white Santa hat instead of a chauffeur's cap.

The driver grinned. "Big Jim's orders," he said. "The boss is like a kid when it comes to Christmas. He likes everybody on his staff to dress the part."

Patricia knelt down to talk to Miranda and Lucy. "What he means," she explained, "is that he's one of Santa's *helpers*. Santa is a very busy man these days, you know!"

The driver whisked their huge stack of luggage into the huge trunk and ushered the Callahans and their pets into the car. Patricia and Gregory were in heaven. They spent the drive to the airport fooling with the sun roof and the DVD player and checking out the mini fridge. Miranda and Lucy made the windows go up and down while they waved to everybody they saw. "Look at us!" they yelled out the window. "We're going to Florida!"

Santa Paws did his best to maintain some dignity, even though the leather seats of the limo were so slippery that he couldn't quite sit up straight. Cookie leapt from side to side, sticking her nose out the window and barking merrily until the driver politely asked the Callahans to "restrain the little black pup, please." And Abigail and Evelyn moaned in protest from within their boxes. They were not the best travelers, but Patricia hoped they'd be fine once the pills took effect. At the hotel, they would have a suite of rooms to roam in, and they'd be as happy as if they were at home.

When they arrived at the airport, the limo drove the Callahans right up to the door of the small purple jet with its cowboy hat emblem. Tipping his Santa hat to them, the driver introduced them to the pilot (who also wore a Santa hat) and wished them a good trip. They traipsed up the small staircase to the jet while helpers in purple-and-white uniforms (and Santa hats!) unloaded their luggage and packed it away.

Patricia couldn't believe her eyes when she saw the inside of the jet. The soft, brown leather seats were arranged around polished wooden tables, with thick, plush beige carpeting underfoot. It felt more like a fancy living room than a plane. There were several other passengers already aboard, as well as two Santa-hatted attendants, but the plane did not feel at all crowded.

"It's like a dream," Patricia said to her aunt Emily, as they buckled themselves into their seats. The Callahans had settled into two groupings of four seats apiece, each pair facing across a table. Gregory and Patricia sat at a table with their parents, and their cousins sat across from them with Steve and Emily. Santa Paws and Cookie had their own space near the front of the cabin, where they were securely belted in for takeoff. The cats were in their carriers, which were placed in cubbyholes so they couldn't slide around.

"Unbelievable," Emily agreed, as the jet taxied down the runway and took off. "Look, girls," she said to her daughters. She pointed out the window. "See the ocean?" Tiny wavelets still showed on the Atlantic, far below them.

"Cool!" said Miranda.

Lucy just stared. It was her very first time on an airplane.

Santa Paws had been on an airplane before —and it had not been a happy trip. He whined as the plane took off, and Gregory tried to comfort him. "It's OK, boy," he said, from his seat. To Patricia, he murmured, "I bet I know what *he's* thinking about."

Patricia nodded and looked over at Steve. No doubt all four of them, Steve, Patricia, Gregory,

31

and Santa Paws, were having the same memory. Years ago, Steve had been piloting a small plane, flying his niece and nephew and their dog to Vermont for the Christmas holidays. The plane had crashed in the middle of New Hampshire's White Mountains, and Steve had been badly hurt. Gregory and Patricia were only eleven and thirteen at the time, and Santa Paws had helped them find their way through the thick woods and deep snow to get help. Santa Paws had been a real hero during that adventure, and nobody in the Callahan family would ever forget it!

Now, the captain was announcing that they were free to walk around the cabin. "Let's untie Santa Paws," Patricia said to Gregory. "Maybe he'll be more comfortable if he can move around for a while." She unbuckled her seat belt and went over to unhook the ties that held Santa Paws and Cookie. As soon he was free, Santa Paws gave himself a happy shake and started to walk toward Gregory.

Just then, the plane gave a lurch.

Whoa! Santa Paws did not like the way the floor beneath his feet kept moving. He froze in his tracks for a moment. Was it safe? He glanced around the plane. Then Gregory called his name. "Hey, big guy! Over here!" Gregory did not sound upset, so everything must be OK. Santa Paws trotted over and lay his big head on Gregory's lap, hoping for an ear scratch.

Meanwhile, Cookie romped over to Miranda and began doing her tricks, hoping for a treat.

A well-dressed woman on the other side of the cabin watched the dogs with a frown on her face. "Really!" she sniffed. "I feel as if I'm with a traveling circus! Can't something be done about these—*animals*?"

One of the attendants, a thin man with red hair, caught Patricia's eye and smiled reassuringly. "It's OK," he mouthed to her. Then he went over to the woman and whispered in her ear. Patricia had the feeling he was telling her about Steve's heroism, judging by the way the woman turned to stare at Steve. She never spoke up again, even when Cookie began doing one of her twirling dance routines in the middle of the aisle.

The rest of the trip seemed to zip by, despite Patricia's wish that this luxury could last forever. "Another bottled water, Ms. Callahan?" the attendant kept asking. "Would you like a pillow or a blanket? How about some chocolates?"

It was a smooth ride—until they began their descent toward the small airport where they would be landing.

At first, the plane just seemed to bounce and tilt slightly. Patricia reminded herself that air turbulence was usually no big deal. She glanced at the red-haired attendant to see if he seemed calm. He was whistling as he put away the remains of the delicious lunch they had been served. Patricia and Gregory got up to make sure Santa Paws and Cookie were safely buckled in and the cats' boxes were secure.

Soon after they sat back down, the plane lurched again—and again. Patricia saw the attendant find his way to a seat and buckle himself in, just as the pilot came over the loudspeaker to announce, "Folks, I'm afraid we're in for some rough weather. There are heavy thunderstorms in the area. Please remain seated and keep your seat belts on. There's no need to panic."

Patricia tried to believe him. She saw that Gregory's face was white and his hands were gripping his armrest. He was scared, too.

"It'll be all right, it'll be all right," Patricia muttered to herself. Just then, there was a *crack!* and a jagged flash of lightning, right outside the window.

4

The plane seemed to tilt hard to the right, and then to the left. Suddenly, it felt as if their small aircraft was no more than a leaf in the wind, twisting and twirling whichever way the storm demanded.

Miranda let out a shriek. "Mommy!" she cried. "I'm scared!"

Patricia knew exactly how her cousin felt. She wished she could jump into her own mommy's lap and hide away from the storm. But she wasn't six years old. She was seventeen. So she just closed her eyes and bit her lip and wished as hard as she could that everything would be all right.

"We'll be OK, honey," Emily soothed her daughter. "The pilot knows what he's doing."

Patricia hoped that was true. What did they know about the pilot, after all? He could just be some old Texas cowboy friend of Big Jim's. She could just hear him saying, "Hey, let me drive one o' them planes, will ya, buddy?"

But the attendant on Patricia's left, the red-haired man, spoke up. "Your mom is right," he told Miranda. "Captain Blodgett has been flying this route for twenty years, through every kind of weather you can imagine. He's the best."

That made Patricia feel better. She glanced at her mom and dad and noticed that they were holding hands. Mom's eyes were closed and her lips were just a tight, white line. Eileen Callahan was not all that fond of flying to begin with, but Patricia knew her mother had decided this trip was worth the anxiety. Now she didn't look so sure.

Dad's brow was sweaty, but other than that he looked his normal, relaxed self. It took a lot to get Dad upset. He met Patricia's eyes and gave her an encouraging smile.

Steve and Emily were holding hands, too. Steve looked, as always, ready to bolt into action. He was great in an emergency. Emily gazed helplessly at her daughters, who were sobbing in fear. They were both terrified of lightning. "It's OK, my sweeties," she said, as the plane lurched and bumped through a lightning-filled sky.

Santa Paws whimpered and Cookie whined, and the low, moaning sound of cats in distress emerged from Abigail and Evelyn's carriers.

Patricia glanced around the plane. The other passengers looked frightened, too. The woman who had complained about the dogs was sitting with eyes tightly shut, clutching her fancy pocketbook to her chest. Her husband sat next to her, his face a mask of fear. Patricia could see droplets of sweat rolling down his white face.

Bump!

Lurch!

The plane tilted side-to-side, then began to dive, nose first. Patricia felt as if she were on a roller coaster. Her stomach flipped as she grabbed for Gregory's hand. So what if he teased her later? She needed to hold on to someone.

Gregory took her hand and squeezed it in his own. When she looked over at him, he was staring back at her, eyes wide. "I can't believe it," he whispered hoarsely. "Not again!" Patricia knew he was thinking about that awful crash so many years ago.

The plane dove straight downward. It seemed as if they *must* be about to crash. The cabin was silent now. Miranda and Lucy had stopped sobbing, the dogs had stopped whining, and even the cats had quit their awful yowling.

Patricia gripped Gregory's hand harder, harder.

And then . . .

Suddenly, the plane was level again. The lurching had stopped. The storm was over. No more lightning. No more bumps. Just cloudy skies that were already parting to show a brilliant, bright blue afternoon.

"Sorry about that, folks," came the pilot's calm

voice over the loudspeaker. "That was a hum-
dinger of a storm! But we're fine now, and we
should be landing shortly. The weather is behind
us and there's nothing but clear skies in the forecast from here on."

Patricia let go of Gregory's hand and leaned
back in her seat, letting out a huge sigh of relief.

Then Santa Paws began to bark.

Now, Santa Paws had lots of different barks.
Patricia knew them all: there was the bark that
meant, "Play with me!" and the bark that said,
"Someone's at the door!" and the bark that could
be translated as, "Where's my dinner?"

Patricia sat straight up in her seat. So did Gregory. They knew this bark, too. It meant, "Something's wrong!" "Danger!" "Trouble!"

Patricia looked at Santa Paws. He was staring
straight toward the woman who had complained
about him. Actually, he was staring at the woman's husband. The man was slumped over in his
seat!

The woman hadn't even noticed because her
eyes were still shut tight. When she heard Santa
Paws bark, she opened her eyes and rolled them
skyward, as if she were about to complain again.
But then she saw her husband, and she began to
scream. "Harry! Harry! Wake up!"

Patricia and Uncle Steve were already unbuck-
ling their seat belts. Patricia had taken a CPR

class as part of her first aid training. That meant she could help with artificial respiration and resuscitation, techniques that could help save a life in the case of a heart attack—which was what this looked like.

"Grab the AED," yelled the red-haired attendant. The other attendant pulled a small, suitcase-shaped case off a bracket on the wall of the plane and dashed over to the man's seat.

Patricia knew that an AED was an automatic defibrillator, a machine that could help when a person's heart wasn't beating right. She and Steve helped the attendants lower the man to the floor and unbutton his shirt so that they could apply the electrodes from the machine. It would analyze his heartbeat and give his heart a shock to make it beat regularly again, if needed. The machine did all that automatically. It even knew how to tell the humans when to "stand clear!" while it delivered the shock.

"OK," said Steve. "It's all hooked up." He pressed a button.

One shock.

Two.

The third time the machine shocked the man, his eyes opened slowly as his breathing returned to normal. "What happened?" he asked, in a daze.

"I think you may have had a heart attack," Steve told him. "Fortunately, our dog noticed that you were no longer conscious, and quick action on the part of these excellent attendants helped save your life."

"He's right," said the man's wife. "That's exactly true! The dog was the one who let us know!" Tears sprung into her eyes as she clutched her husband. "Oh, Harry! That dog is an angel! A true angel!"

Patricia had to suppress a smile, picturing Santa Paws wearing a halo, wings spread out behind him.

"We'd better get back to our seats," said an attendant. "We've begun our final descent. We'll land in just a few minutes. I'll radio in to make sure there's an ambulance waiting for you," he told the man. "You'll still need to go to the hospital and have a full checkup."

On the way back to her seat, Patricia stopped to give Santa Paws a big hug and a kiss. "You did it again," she whispered into his soft, silky ear. "Good boy."

A half hour later, Patricia and her family climbed out of another stretch limo and walked—in a bit of a daze—up to the grand entranceway of The Oasis.

It had been an exciting drive from the airport over the long bridge and onto the island. The air in Florida was warm and moist and full of flowery, sweet smells. Bright blossoms in tropical

40

colors spilled over every embankment along the highway, and tall palm trees lined the streets of Christmas Island. They passed all sorts of "Now-I-*Know*-I'm-in-Florida" sights, like a gift shop in the shape of a giant conch shell, the Pirate's Lair restaurant, and Smithie's Alligator Farm.

When the limo pulled up to The Oasis, Patricia drew in a breath. The place looked like a mirage, with its shimmering white towers and rows of pillars. Every tree and shrub was draped in tiny white lights for the holidays.

"I see three—no, four—pools!" Gregory whispered, as they drove through the beautifully-landscaped grounds of the hotel, which faced its own private beach.

"And a water slide!" Miranda shouted.

"There's plenty to do here," said their Santa-hatted driver. "You aren't going to be bored, I can guarantee that."

When they arrived at the front desk, which was draped in evergreens and decorated with big red satin bows, they were greeted by a handsome, black-haired man in a Santa hat. He didn't raise an eyebrow at the sight of the raggle-taggle family and their pets.

"Welcome, welcome," he said, giving Cookie a pat as she nosed at his shiny shoes. "I'm Donald Kent, the manager, and you must be the Callahans. We've been told to expect you. Mr. Jessup instructed us to extend every courtesy to you and your pets. We have some lovely suites reserved for your use." He started punching keys on his computer

"Oh, we don't need anything fancy —" began Mrs. Callahan. But she stopped when Mr. Callahan elbowed her.

"That will be swell," he said grandly. "Lead the way!"

"We're just putting the finishing touches on our welcome service in your rooms," said Mr. Kent. "Please feel free to explore the lobby and grounds, and your suites should be ready in a few minutes. You may want to check out our activity boards, so you can plan what you would most like to do during your stay." He saw Mrs. Callahan's worried look and smiled. "Of course, all activities are free for you, as guests of Big Jim."

"All right!" said Gregory. "I know what I want to do. Are there surfing lessons?"

"Certainly," said Mr. Kent. "Take a look at our bulletin board, and you'll see that we offer group lessons every morning."

"Yay!" said Miranda. "I want to do that, too!"

"Well," began her mother.

"Lessons are for all ages over five!" said Mr. Kent. "Some local children start surfing as soon as they can walk."

"I'll keep an eye on her," Gregory promised. He smiled down at Miranda. "This'll be a blast," he said. He had always wanted to learn to surf, but somehow he had never gotten around to it, even though he'd spent his life near the ocean. The water in Rhode Island was pretty cold and Gregory didn't have a wetsuit.

Patricia wasn't sure what she wanted to do, besides sit by the pool or on the beach. She wandered blissfully through the lobby, admiring the stunning Christmas decorations, which included the tallest Christmas tree she'd ever seen, covered in twinkling white lights. Then she gazed at the bulletin board to see what activites were offered. As she was looking at a sign-up sheet for beach volleyball, she caught a movement out of the corner of her eye and turned to see a *very* handsome boy, with sandy hair that fell into his deep blue eyes. He had a dark, golden tan. He was pinning up a notice on the board, and he gave her a big, gorgeous smile when he saw her looking.

"Join us!" he said.

"I will," she answered, automatically. "Count me in!" Anything this boy was doing would *have* to be fun.

It wasn't until he had turned and left that Patricia had a chance to find out what she had signed on for. She took a look at the notice, which was decorated with red and blue beach umbrella sketches. The headline read:

BEACH PARTY WITH THE CHRISTMAS ISLAND
ENVIRONMENTAL CLUB!

Cool, Patricia thought. A party sounded like

an excellent way to get to know Christmas Island — and at least one of its very attractive citizens. She leaned closer to see the smaller type.

HELP US CLEAN UP THE BEACH,
MEET AT SIX A.M. AT THE OASIS LIFEGUARD STAND.
BRING YOUR OWN GARBAGE BAG!

5

Patricia groaned when the phone on her bedside table rang at five-thirty the next morning. "Hello?" she croaked groggily, picking it up.

"This is the wake-up call you requested," said a cheery voice. "Good morning, Ms. Callahan!"

"Right," Patricia said. "Thanks." She let the phone fall back into the cradle and rolled over, wishing she could just slide back into the dream she'd been having about swimming with dolphins. That was something she'd wanted to do for as long as she could remember. It always sounded so magical. She was hoping her dream might come true during this Christmas Island vacation—but first, she had a job to do.

Beach cleanup. Yeesh.

It wasn't like Patricia was against clean beaches. She considered herself a total environmentalist. She recycled her magazines and catalogs, used earth-friendly detergents, and never, ever littered. But still, rising before dawn to pick up garbage was not exactly her idea of the best way to kick off her first-ever Florida vacation.

Then she remembered those deep blue eyes and that sandy hair.

Right. She knew there was a reason she'd promised to do this!

Patricia threw back her light blanket and looked around her room with satisfaction. Now *this* was a first-class hotel room! This was the kind of place where celebrities stayed.

The room was decorated in shades of white, accented with pink. The carpet was thick white shag, the walls were ivory, and the sheer curtains across the huge picture window shimmered like mother-of-pearl on the inside of a shell. There was a dresser made of bamboo, and a small bamboo dressing table with a bamboo chair. Patricia had her own bathroom, with a deep whirlpool tub and plush white towels embroidered with a sweeping script *O* framing three palm trees, the logo of The Oasis.

A door across from Patricia's bed led into the "sitting room" of the suite she shared with Gregory. That room had a beautiful seating area with cushy upholstered chairs in shades of pink and cream, as well as a bamboo dining table with a glass top, flanked by two bamboo chairs. There was a full entertainment center by the seating area, with a giant flat-screen TV. Normally Patricia would have been thrilled by that—but here in Florida she knew she'd much rather spend her time on the beach and in the water than sitting in a room, no matter how beautiful, watching TV.

Patricia got out of bed, rubbing her eyes, and pulled on her purple Speedo and a pair of capri pants. She threw on an Oceanport High T-shirt just in case it was still cool outside, and slipped into her purple flip-flops. Grabbing her sunglasses and sunscreen, she poked her head into the sitting room to see if Santa Paws wanted to come with her. Gregory had left his bedroom door open so the dog would have more room to wander. Sure enough, Santa Paws rose to his feet as soon as he saw her. He was eager to explore this new place.

She clipped on his leash. "Let's hit the beach, sweet pea," she said, using the nickname Gregory hated. They headed for the door.

The lobby of The Oasis was quiet as Patricia and Santa Paws walked through. Not too many vacationers got up *this* early.

Now that she was more awake, Patricia felt proud of herself. Naturally, she would love to sleep in while she was on vacation, like Gregory and the rest of her family. But she had more important issues on her mind. Patricia Callahan was a person who truly cared about the environment. She wasn't the type who would just come to some tourist spot and lie in the sun. Oh, no. Patricia was a girl with integrity, with values. She believed in doing her part to make the world a better place, even while she was on vacation.

So—where *was* that cute guy?

Patricia walked out onto the beach and looked around. The sun was just coming up, and the sky looked like a painting, all pink and gold and blue. Waves crashed on the shore while seagulls squawked and whirled overhead. The sand was cool and soft beneath Patricia's feet. Looking down, she immediately spotted the prettiest shell she had ever seen. She bent to pick it up.

"Well, hello," said a voice behind her.

Was that him? Patricia turned to see a boy coming toward her. And he was—unbelievably—even *cuter* than the one she expected to see! This boy had dark shaggy brown hair and eyes the color of green sea glass, set in a ruddy brown face with a quirky, crooked smile. He wore a whistle around his neck, a bright red vest with the word LIFEGUARD in white on the back, and a Santa hat—which somehow only made him look even cuter.

"Uh—hi!" said Patricia.

"You're out early," he said. "I'm Jax. Jackson Turner. Everybody calls me Jax, though." He stuck out his hand for a shake. "You staying at The Oasis?"

She nodded, shaking his hand automatically. The Santa hat meant this boy worked for Big Jim

48

Jessup. "Patricia," she managed to squeak out. "And this is Santa Paws."

"Haven't I heard that name before?" Jax reached out to give Santa Paws a pat. "Is he some kind of celebrity?"

"Well," Patricia began, "sort of." It was true that lots of people had heard of Santa Paws and his talent for rescuing people in trouble.

"Are you two always up and out at dawn?"

Patricia laughed. "No way," she said. "But I said I'd help with—" she held up the empty garbage bag she was carrying. She had "borrowed" it from a trash can in the hotel hallway when she remembered at the last minute that she was supposed to bring one.

"Ah!" Jax nodded. "You're joining the enviro-geeks."

Patricia's cheeks grew hot. Was he making fun of her? "I—"

"Just kidding," said Jax quickly. "Everybody appreciates the work they do. But I get my kicks surfing the big waves and, occasionally, saving lives." He gave a mock bow. "In fact," he went on, "I'm out here early to scout the waves. Hope to ride a few later on!" Then he flashed her a crooked smile. "Have fun!" he said, as he hoisted himself up onto a tall, white lifeguard chair that was painted with The Oasis's palm-tree logo.

Patricia shaded her eyes and looked at him sitting up there. What a great job! She could just imagine it. Sitting up on that chair all day, looking out at the waves, getting a great tan . . .

"Hey, you made it!"

Patricia turned to see the sandy-haired boy smiling at her. He wore a faded red Earth Day T-shirt and ragged cutoffs, and his eyes were a perfect match for the blue of the ocean.

She smiled back and held up her garbage bag. "I'm here!" she said. "Ready to work."

"Brought your pup, too. That's great! This is one of the few local beaches where dogs are allowed. Good thing Big Jim Jessup is a dog lover."

"This is Santa Paws," Patricia said. "And I'm Patricia."

"Good to meet both of you. I'm Thomas." He waved at someone behind her. "And there's the rest of the gang."

Patricia turned to see a cluster of people, all holding garbage bags. She and Thomas walked over to meet them, and he introduced her around. It was an interesting group, ranging in age from little kids to a woman named Esther who Patricia thought looked about her grandmother's age.

They fanned out and walked slowly down the beach, picking up any litter they spotted. There wasn't a lot, but Patricia was surprised at what they found: cigarette butts, fast-food containers, soda cans. Santa Paws had a great talent for spotting bits of garbage that nobody else noticed; he padded along carrying a Styrofoam coffee cup in his mouth. As they walked, Thomas told Patricia about all the work the environmental club did. "You should be here when the sea turtles are laying eggs," he said. "We've saved so many hatchlings. Nothing beats the feeling of watching one of those tiny turtles swim safely into the surf."

"Have you ever gone swimming with dolphins?" Patricia asked him. She had a feeling Thomas would understand her dream.

He nodded. "Oh, yeah," he said. "I've done it lots of times. It's incredible! You really feel like you're communicating with them." He stopped and looked at her. "Want to go with me sometime?"

"Absolutely," said Patricia, staring into his deep, blue eyes.

Meanwhile, far down the beach, Gregory and Miranda were just arriving for their first surfing lesson. "This is going to be so totally-otally awesome!" Miranda said, skipping along the beach next to Gregory.

"You're not kidding, amigo, " Gregory agreed. "I am so stoked!"

He could picture himself riding a huge crystal-clear green wave capped with a pure white crest. People on the beach would be speechless at the sight. Nobody on Christmas Island had ever surfed *that* break before! A photographer from the *Christmas Island Crier*, the local newspaper, would click away as Gregory's triumphant ride came to an end. When he emerged from the water, girls in bikinis would rush over to get his autograph.

That would be later, though, after a lesson or two. Now, Gregory and Miranda were approaching a knot of about six little girls in bathing suits, ranging from Miranda's age to maybe eleven years old. They were all whispering and giggling as Gregory and Miranda drew near. Pests, thought Gregory. It was not the first time he had realized how lucky he was not to have a little sister. Patricia was bad enough.

"Isn't this where the surfing lesson is supposed to meet?" Miranda asked.

"It must be farther up the beach," Gregory said, scanning the shore. He saw nothing but long-legged plovers, black and white birds on stilt-like legs, playing in the wavelets that smoothed the wet sand.

"Surfing?" asked a girl in a turquoise blue tankini. "Yes! That's what we're all here for. The group lesson? It starts in, like, five minutes!" She bounced up and down. "I can't wait!" she squealed.

The other girls started bouncing up and down and squealing, too.

Gregory, who towered at least two feet over the tallest girl, groaned. This was *not* what he had pictured. Suddenly, the image of himself surfing a giant wave evaporated. It was replaced by a picture of himself looking like a foolish giant, surrounded by pygmy-sized girls who pointed at him and giggled. For a second, he thought he might tell Miranda he'd changed his mind, and that he didn't feel like taking a surfing lesson, after all. Then he remembered that he had promised his aunt to keep an eye on his young cousin.

He was trapped.

No doubt the guy teaching the lessons would smirk at him and make him feel even more ridiculous. Oh, well. Gregory could take it. He wouldn't let his embarrassment show. He hiked up his surf trunks, looked out at the waves, and sighed.

"Where's the teacher?" Miranda asked.

Gregory shrugged. "Who knows?" he asked. He couldn't blame the guy for being late. Why would anybody be in a hurry to spend hours trying to teach a gaggle of little girls how to surf?

"There she is!" yelled the girl in the blue tankini.

She? Gregory turned to look.

Whoa. Walking down the beach was a girl who looked as if she'd just stepped out of a surfing poster. She was taller than Gregory and—he gulped—probably twice as strong, with long white-blonde hair. She wore red-and-white flowered surf shorts and a red tank top, and—since she was an Oasis employee—a Santa hat was perched adorably on her head. She carried a huge surfboard under her arm, as easily as if it were a loaf of French bread.

"Yay!" yelled all the girls. "It's Montana!"

Montana. Gregory felt dizzy all of a sudden. Could he have a case of sunstroke? No, it wasn't even near noon.

"Hey," said the surfer girl, as she approached the group. She put down her board and tossed her hair over her shoulder. "So, who's ready to rock and roll?"

"We are!" chorused the girls at top volume.

Gregory just gulped again.

6

"**M**ore orange juice, Tom?" Emily Callahan passed the glass pitcher to her brother-in-law. The four Callahan adults were having breakfast in the sitting room of the suite they shared. This suite had three bedrooms: one for Steve and Emily, one for Tom and Eileen, and one for Miranda and Lucy. The bedrooms opened into a living room area like Patricia and Gregory's, only this one was even larger and more luxurious.

Abigail and Evelyn seemed completely at home. They'd decided, as cats will do, that the place was theirs and that they were being generous to let the humans share it. Abigail lounged on top of the media center, her tail twitching back and forth across the TV screen on which Lucy was watching cartoons. Evelyn was curled up on the couch next to Lucy, one eye open in case Lucy decided to attack her. In Evelyn's experience, small children were completely unpredictable. One minute they could be petting you gently, the next they might be pulling on your tail. And if you dared to even *threaten* to scratch one of these precious humans, you'd likely find yourself shut up in the bathroom with no dinner. Evelyn had learned to restrain the urge to educate these unformed beings in the correct way to relate to cats. She was proud of herself for that.

Cookie sat at Lucy's feet, well out of Evelyn's reach but close enough to be in perfect position to scarf up any graham-cracker crumbs that Lucy dropped. Cookie had lived with little girls long enough to know that staying close meant plenty of chances at spilled food. It was worth putting up with occasional tail-tugging incidents, in her opinion.

Tom Callahan smiled contentedly as he poured himself a tall glass of juice from the pitcher Emily had passed him. "Fresh squeezed!" he said. "Only the best. This place really does breakfast right." He reached for another fresh, warm cinnamon bun from the basket on the table. "It's going to be a snap to write this article."

"Still, honey, you should probably get started on it today, don't you think?" his wife asked, frowning as she watched him bite into the roll. It was his third. "Christmas is just around the corner, you know."

"That's right," he said. "I'll make a few notes. Nothing bad to say, that's for sure! The bed is the most comfortable I've ever slept on, the bathroom is deluxe, the food is excellent." As he spoke, he lifted the silver domed lid that was keeping a plate of food warm. Room service had delivered a huge breakfast, and it was hard to keep track of everything. "Ah, my omelet!" he said, peeking under the lid. "It looks perfect."

He peeked under another silver dome. "Well, well, well," he said, smiling. "Look what we have here!" He grinned at his brother. "Your friend Big Jim believes in treating *all* his guests right." He lifted the lid off. On the plate were a small box of Milk-Bones, two pouches of cat treats, plus a home style oatmeal-raisin cookie. "I think I know who these are for," said Mr. Callahan. "We'll save the Milk-Bones for you-know-who. Cookie! Want a treat? Psst, Abigail and Evelyn—you, too!"

The pets ran over and accepted their goodies eagerly.

"Well, the pool is calling me!" said Eileen Callahan, as she took one last sip of coffee. She stood up and stretched. "What do you say, Em? Ready to start our Pool Survey?"

The two sisters-in-law had decided to spend time at each of The Oasis's pools. They were going to start with the Aloha pool, which was landscaped with orchids, birds-of-paradise, and other tropical flowers. They planned to rate all the pools, awarding points for things like "good people watching" and "best pool chairs." They would pass their "research" on to Tom, for his article, since Mr. Callahan was not one for lounging by the pool. Or on the beach, for that matter. He believed firmly in shade and air-conditioning as the best ways to enjoy Florida's heat, and intended to spend as much of his time as possible communing with Abigail and Evelyn in their beautiful suite.

"This pool research is going to be brutally hard work, but somebody has to do it," Emily said now, with a pretend sigh. She reached for her tote bag, which held three magazines and two books she couldn't wait to read. "I'm ready when you are."

"And I'm ready to hit the beach with Lucy and Cookie," said Steve. "Ready to do some beach-combing, kiddo?" he asked his younger daughter, sweeping her up for a tickle.

"Yes!" she yelled. "I get sunglasses!" She dashed into her room to rummage in her backpack for the red, heart-shaped sunglasses her cousin Patricia had given her. She dashed back into the room with the oversize specs slipping down her nose. Her frilly red bathing suit was a perfect match. "Let's catch some rays, Daddy!" she cried.

Meanwhile, out on the beach, Gregory was surfing! Well, not quite. He was wearing surf shorts. He was standing on a surfboard. He was balancing with his arms out in that cool surfer way. He would *totally* have been surfing except for one thing: He wasn't actually in the water yet. He and his classmates were still practicing on shore. Apparently, that was Lesson One for new surfers, or "grommets" as Montana smilingly called her students.

"OK, dudes," she'd said, once introductions were over. She led them to a row of surfboards that lay waiting in the sand. "Let's play Get to Know Your Board! Everybody grab a board and we'll go over the basics."

Gregory and Miranda chose boards near the end of the row and watched as Montana went over the parts of a surfboard. "This," she said, pointing at the top of her board, "is the nose. The other end is the tail. And that thing that sticks down into the water at the tail end is known as a skeg, or fin. It keeps your board sliding straight when you're riding a wave."

Gregory nodded. All the little girls nodded, too.

"Got that? Great." Montana went on. "The top of the board, the part you stand on, is the deck. And the sides of the board," she ran her hands along the sides, "are known as the rails. So if I tell you to grab the rails, you'll know what I mean, right?"

"Right!" everybody yelled.

"Awesome. The last thing I want to show you is your leash," Montana said. She held up a length of rope with a Velcro strap attached. "How many of you have dogs?"

Miranda jumped up and down and waved her hand, along with four other girls. "I do! I do!" they yelled. Gregory just raised a finger, trying to act a bit cooler and more mature.

"So, you know what a leash is, right? It keeps you attached to your dog. Well, guess what a surfboard leash does?"

"Keeps you attached to your surfboard?" guessed Miranda.

"Bingo!" said Montana. "And that's important. If you wipe out or lose hold of your board, you don't want it to go shooting through the waves by itself. It could hit another surfer and that can hurt somebody bad." She demonstrated how to use the leash, attaching the Velcro strap to her ankle and clipping the end of the rope to a plug on her board. "That's how it works! Simple." Then she stood up straight and held out her arms. "That's it! Surfboards 101. There's more to learn about the different types of boards and what they're each best for, but that's all you need to know right now."

"Great!" said Gregory. "So do we get to surf now?" He had been watching the glassy green waves roll toward shore, and he could hardly wait to jump in.

Montana laughed. "Well, not quite yet," she said. "I have to explain a few things first. Then we'll practice our pop-ups. *Then* we'll get wet."

"Pop-ups?" Gregory asked.

"Here's how it works," Montana said. "To catch

a wave, first you paddle out on your board, to a spot beyond where the waves are breaking." She paused. "'Breaking' means when the wave crashes over and there's white foam at the top." She looked around the circle. "Got that?"

The girls—and Gregory—nodded.

"OK, so you'll most likely be lying on your stomach to paddle out, using your hands as flippers." Montana went on with her explanation. "When you see a wave you want to ride, you're going to turn your board back toward shore. Then you're going to have to figure out how to stand up since that's how you want to be riding the wave, right?" She nodded in answer to her own question. "That's where pop-ups come in."

She lay down on her own board, right there in the sand. "Paddle, paddle, paddle," she said, making paddling motions with her hands. "Turn around. And—" She grabbed the board's rails and jumped up to a low squat with her feet beneath her body. Then she rose slowly, arms out to the sides for balance and knees bent, "—pop-up!" she cried, as she pretended to ride a wave.

"Yay!" yelled all the girls, clapping their hands.

Montana stepped off her board and gave a quick curtsy. "Thank you, thank you," she said. "You've seen how it's done. Now, you try it."

Gregory felt silly lying on his board in the sand, pretending to paddle. But he did it gamely. He didn't want Montana to think he was a spoilsport.

"Paddle, paddle, paddle," directed Montana. "Now, pop-up!"

Ten little girls jumped up and landed perfectly squarely on their boards.

One tall sixteen-year-old boy jumped up and landed on his butt in the sand.

"Oops!" Montana covered her mouth, but Gregory could see it in her eyes: She was giggling. He didn't mind that so much—after all, he probably looked pretty funny, sprawled in the sand. But what he *did* mind was that a bunch of guys chose that very moment to walk by. Surfer guys. With tans and cool board shorts and surfboards under their arms. And they were snickering.

"Slick move, dude!" said one of them, a gangly guy with black hair.

"Oh, keep it to yourself, G-Dog," said Montana. "You were a grommet once, too."

"Maybe," said the boy. "But I never had a dry-land wipeout." He snickered again.

Montana gave him a fierce look.

He stopped snickering. "See ya," he said. "Gotta meet Jax. Come on out and catch some waves with us when you're done with these grommets." He waved and sauntered on down the beach with his buds.

Montana turned to Gregory and shrugged. "Sorry," she said.

"G-Dog?" Gregory asked. "That guy's name is G-Dog?"

Montana shrugged again. "Surfers have pretty funny names sometimes," she said.

Gregory nodded, remembering a snowboarder he knew named Frogger.

"Ready to try again?" Montana asked.

"Sure," Gregory said. For the next half hour, he and the girls practiced pop-up after pop-up, until Gregory was hot and sweaty and covered with sand.

"Yeah!" said Montana, coming around to watch Gregory. He had finally mastered the pop-up and was nailing it nearly every time. "That's it!" She studied his foot placement. "Ha, you're a goofy foot, like me."

Gregory wasn't offended. He knew what she meant. "I'm goofy on my snowboard, too," he told her. That meant that he liked to keep his right foot forward on the board, the opposite of the way most people rode.

"Cool." Montana nodded. "I always wanted to try boarding. You know, I've never even seen snow."

Gregory would have liked the conversation to continue, but Miranda interrupted. "So, can we go in the water now?" she begged Montana.

"Definitely," said Montana. "Let's go catch some waves!" She led her class down to a spot where small waves flowed into the shore. "We'll start with these," she said. "Monster waves come later."

Soon the whole class was paddling out, turning their boards, and waiting for just the right moment to pop up and ride a wave back to shore. It was not *anywhere* as easy as Gregory had thought it would be. No matter how hard he tried, he couldn't get up into a standing position before falling over one way or another. Once, he almost got it—but he was standing too far forward on his board and the nose dove under, dunking him in the salty green water.

After a while, he gave up and started working with Miranda. He saw how Montana was helping the other girls get into a standing position, and he coached his cousin the same way.

Unlike Gregory, Miranda was a natural. "Look at me!" she yelled, as she jumped up and rode a wave for several feet.

"Eeek!" she cried, as she tumbled off the board and into the water. She came up quickly, sneezing salt water and laughing.

There was applause from shore where Steve, Cookie, and Lucy stood watching.

Cookie didn't understand. How could everybody be smiling and laughing when Miranda was in trouble? Miranda needed help. She needed help now!

Cookie plunged into the water.

"No, Cookie!" Steve yelled. "Come back! Miranda's fine!" He ran after the dog but didn't quite catch her. Cookie swam to Miranda, grabbed her by the bathing suit, and started to tow her back toward shore.

Steve watched and laughed, shaking his head over the dog's antics. Then he plodded back up the beach to Lucy.

But Lucy wasn't there.

7

Lucy didn't *mean* to wander off. She only meant to get closer to the yellow and green ball some bigger kids were playing with, a little way down the beach. It was a big ball. The biggest ball in the *world*, probably. And Lucy wanted to be near it. Thumb stuck firmly in her mouth, she shuffled down the beach. Sand collected inside her red sandals, but she didn't really mind. Her eyes were on the ball.

"Watch out!" a boy called.

Suddenly, the ball was bouncing in Lucy's direction—*fast*! It was kind of scary, like a big monster running toward her. Lucy froze for a moment, then ran as fast as her chubby, short legs could carry her—away from the ball.

That was when she spotted the ice-cream lady. Mmm! Ice cream! Suddenly Lucy couldn't think of anything except an orange Popsicle, her favorite. She ran faster, trying to catch up with the ice-cream lady.

Meanwhile her father was not feeling nearly so happy. "Lucy!" Steve yelled. He whirled around, scanning the beach in all directions. Where was she? He'd only had his back turned for a few moments. How could she have disappeared so quickly?

Now that the sun was high in the sky, there were lots of people on the beach. Some lounged under umbrellas near the hotel's cabanas—a row of red-and-white striped canvas tents where you could change clothes—while others played beach volleyball or just sprawled in the sand. The sky was a deep, cloudless blue, and the palm trees lining the beach danced in a light breeze.

It was a perfect Florida scene on a perfect Florida day.

Except for one thing.

Lucy was missing.

"Lucy!" Steve called again. "Come on, sweetie! Where are you?" Lucy and Miranda had been playing lots of hide-and-seek lately. Maybe Lucy was waiting for him to call "Olly olly oxen free!" so she could run out of her hiding place.

Steve cleared his throat. Well, why not? "Olly olly oxen free!" he yelled, as loudly as he could. "Come on, Lucy! Game's over!"

People turned to stare at him, but Steve didn't care. Where was his little girl? He yelled again. "Olly olly oxen free!"

Lucy didn't hear him. She was far off down

the beach. She had lost the ice-cream lady in the crowd, but then she had seen a funny bird, running on long legs and making a *peep-peep*! sound. Lucy remembered when she went to the chicken farm with Nonee, her pre-school teacher. They had seen tiny fluffy baby chicks that ran around making the same sound. Nonee had picked one up and let Lucy pet it. Maybe this time Lucy could pick up her *own* bird. She ran after it, stumbling through the sand. All this running was making her tired.

Back up the beach, Steve yelled the hide-and-seek phrase one more time, feeling silly. Cookie's ears perked up. She knew that sound. Miranda said those words all the time when she and Lucy were playing. Cookie and Santa Paws liked to play hide-and-seek, too. It was always fun to run around poking your nose behind couches or underneath beds, hoping to turn up a squealing little girl.

"Um, can I help you, sir?"

Steve turned to see a boy in a red vest and a Santa hat, with a whistle around his neck. It was the Oasis lifeguard. Steve had seen him up on his chair when he and Lucy first arrived at the beach. Now the boy was looking at him as if he were a crazy person. "It's my daughter," Steve told the boy. "She's missing."

The boy nodded. "I'm Jax," he said. "I'll help you find her." He blew his whistle and yelled for everyone to get out of the water. "Just a safety measure," he assured Steve.

Then he reached into his vest pocket and pulled out a walkie-talkie. "Calling all lifeguards!" he said. "Missing child alert. Stand by for description." He looked at Steve, eyebrows raised. "What does she look like?"

"She's three," said Steve. "Curly blond hair. Blue eyes. Red bathing suit and red baseball cap. Big smile."

As Jax was repeating the description into his radio, Gregory and Miranda came running out of the water. "What's up, Uncle Steve?" Gregory asked.

"Lucy!" said Steve. "She disappeared."

"What?" Miranda asked. She looked scared.

Steve tried to reassure his daughter. "I'm sure she's right around here somewhere," he said. "She can't have gone far. I only had my back turned for a second, when Cookie dove in after you."

"We'll help look," said Gregory immediately.

"I thought she might be playing hide-and-seek," said Steve. "So I was yelling for her to come out. But it doesn't look as if she heard me."

"She's getting to be a very good hider," Miranda said thoughtfully. "But she always comes out if you call."

"Does she know how to swim?" Jax had finished talking on the radio.

Steve's face turned white. "She's only three,"

he said. He glanced out at the ocean. It looked awfully big all of a sudden.

"Don't worry," Jax said quickly. "I doubt she would go in the water. Anyway, there are lifeguards all the way up and down the beach. Everybody is keeping an eye out for her."

"Cookie will help us," said Miranda. "Right, Cookie? Find Lucy! Find her!"

Cookie knew this game. She *loved* this game. She stuck her nose into the air and sniffed deeply, sorting through hundreds of unfamiliar smells and hoping to sense one she recognized. She tilted her head and listened as hard as she could. Then, suddenly, she took off running.

Gregory didn't even stop to think. He ran right after her.

Lucy would have been surprised at all the fuss. She was perfectly happy. She had followed the bird way out on a long, curving pier made of big rocks, but then the bird had flown away. Now she stood watching the waves roll in. Some of them were tiny baby waves. Some were mama waves, a bit bigger. And some were papa waves! They splashed up hard on the rocks Lucy was perched on, making her giggle and squeal.

Far down the beach, Patricia and Thomas were strolling back toward The Oasis, enjoying the tidy look of the shore they had helped to clean up. They were deep in conversation, and hadn't even noticed that the rest of the Christmas Island

Environmental Club had left the beach once the sun had begun to beat down.

"So, do you do a lot of environmental work up there in Rhode Island?" Thomas was asking Patricia.

"Sure," she said. It wasn't a lie. Just last week she had helped her mom take a huge load of stuff to the recycling center. Plus, she remembered, she had recently signed a petition some kids were circulating, about creating a composting area for leftover stuff from school lunches. She told Thomas about that.

"Awesome," he said. "It's great to know that there are activists everywhere."

Patricia bent down to pick up a Popsicle stick they had missed on their way down the beach. "You didn't spot this one, did you, Mr. Big Nose?" she asked Santa Paws, who had been trotting along beside her.

But the dog wasn't listening. Not to Patricia, anyway. He stood still, nose in the air and head cocked. He sniffed. He listened. His muscles quivered in anticipation.

"What is it, Santa Paws?" Patricia knew something was wrong. She could always tell when her dog sensed trouble.

"Wow, what's up with your dog?" Thomas asked.

But Patricia didn't have time to answer. Just then, Santa Paws took off like a streak down the beach, and she took off, too, running after him. For one thing, if there was trouble she wanted to help out. And for another thing, she did not want Santa Paws running off and getting lost in a place that was unfamiliar to him. She realized, too late, that she probably should have kept him on his leash. Not that a leash could hold Santa Paws back when he knew someone was in trouble . . .

Out on the pier, Lucy was still having fun watching the waves. But she was also starting to wonder. Where was her daddy? Where were Miranda, and Cookie, and Santa Paws, and Gregory, and Patricia? They would like watching the waves, too. Why weren't they here? Suddenly, Lucy began to feel very alone out there on the rocky pier. She decided to go back and find everybody. But when she turned around, she saw something funny. Lots of papa waves had come at once, and the rocks behind her were all covered up now! Instead of a rocky trail back to the beach, there was just water flowing back and forth. Lucy looked at it, then turned again and looked toward sea. Even bigger papa waves were coming. What if one of them covered *her* up? Lucy opened her mouth wide and began to wail.

"Santa Paws!" Gregory shouted, when he saw his dog tearing past him. Patricia was following behind him, panting with the effort of running down the hot beach in the midday sun.

Santa Paws didn't stop. He just blasted right past Gregory. Cookie took off with him, and the two dogs raced along the shoreline in tandem.

"What—what is it?" Patricia gasped, when she caught up to Gregory.

"Lucy," Gregory said grimly. "Missing."

"I think *they* know where she is," Patricia said, shading her eyes to watch the dogs disappearing down the beach.

Gregory shaded his eyes, too. "What's that?" he asked. "That splotch of red, out on those rocks?"

Patricia looked. And gasped.

They both took off running.

By the time Gregory and Patricia reached the flooded pier, Santa Paws and Cookie had already plunged into the foamy green waves and were moving fast toward Lucy, half swimming, half walking through the shallow, choppy water. In moments, they had reached her.

"Look, Lucy's grabbed onto his collar, and he's towing her back," Gregory said. Sure enough, Santa Paws had clambered up on the rocks and allowed Lucy to throw her arms around him. Then he had scrambled back down and jumped back into the water. Cookie swam alongside him, her nose up against Lucy as if to comfort the crying girl.

Just then, Jax ran up. "Wow!" he said, as he tore off his vest and Santa hat. "Your dog really is a hero!" Grabbing a flotation device, he ran into the water and helped Santa Paws and Cookie bring Lucy back to shore.

Lucy had stopped crying by the time Patricia and Gregory knelt to hug her. She was a brave little girl, and she knew she was safe now. She kissed Santa Paws and Cookie. Then she kissed Jax. When Steve and Miranda arrived, there were more kisses and hugs.

Patricia would have liked to kiss Jax, too. But instead, she just said, "Thank you!" and gave him a huge smile.

"What's all the fuss about?" Tom Callahan was on the beach by the time they got back. He looked completely out of place in long pants, a long-sleeved shirt, and—Patricia cringed and hoped Jax didn't notice them—bunny slippers. Dad could be so absentminded when he was writing!

"Lucy ran off and got lost," Steve replied. He bent again to give his daughter a squeeze.

"But Cookie and Santa Paws found her," Miranda told her uncle. "Gregory and Patricia helped, too," she added. "And Jax."

Tom pulled a small notebook out of his pocket. He scribbled some notes. "Very dramatic," he said. "Maybe I could use this for my opening paragraph."

"Uh, Dad?" Gregory said. "No offense, but I'm not sure that a lost child is the kind of thing that

Big Jim has in mind to promote his new resort."

Mr. Callahan nodded and sighed. "I guess you're right," he said. "It's just that this story is turning out to be harder than I thought. There's plenty to write about this place, but it's always important to start off with something really dramatic. It's one of those journalism tricks, you know? A snappy lead really 'makes' an article."

"At least you're out and about now," his brother said. "Somehow I don't think a snappy lead is going to turn up if you laze around in our suite all day."

Tom Callahan raised an eyebrow. "Laze around?" he asked. "I'll have you know I've been hard at work. Also, I'm keeping the cats company. Somebody has to do it!"

"Well, we'll take our turn now," said Steve. "I think this one—" he gestured to Lucy "might be ready for a little n-a-p after all that excitement."

"I'm not tired, Daddy!" Lucy protested. She knew what those letters spelled. But she took his right hand, and Miranda took the other, and they headed back to their room.

8

Patricia groaned as she rolled over and stared in disbelief at the clock by her bed. Why was the phone ringing? It was only six A.M.! She *knew* she hadn't asked for another wake-up call. In fact, she had gone to bed feeling very happy about being able to sleep in the next morning. After all, wasn't that part of what vacation was all about? Relaxing?

The night before, the whole family had eaten out at the Pirate's Lair. What a fun restaurant! There was nothing like it back in Oceanport. All the waiters had beards and wore scarves tied around their heads and carried cutlasses at their waists. One waiter even had a real parrot sitting on his shoulder! It said things like, "Order the ribs! They're verrry tasty!"

The parrot was right. The ribs had been delicious, and so had everything else. And the pets had appreciated all the leftovers the family brought back in a doggie bag. (Evelyn *wished* they wouldn't call it that!) Patricia had drifted off to sleep with a smile, knowing she could stay in bed until Santa Paws woke her up for a walk or until she got hungry again, whichever came first.

Instead, her phone was ringing.

Patricia picked up the receiver. "Hello?" she croaked. She expected to hear the female voice she'd heard the day before. Then she could explain that her request for a wake-up call had been for *only* that day.

"Patricia?" It was Thomas!

And he sounded upset. "I'm calling on my cell phone from the beach. Can you come out here? You're not going to believe this."

Patricia frowned. "What's the matter?"

"Just come," said Thomas. "Please?"

"Well—OK." Patricia figured she was already awake. She might as well take Santa Paws out. He was always ready for a walk, the earlier the better. "I'll be there in a few minutes." She hung up the phone and rolled onto her back with a sigh. Santa Paws heard her stirring and came trotting into the room, his collar tags jingling.

Finally, he thought. It was about time somebody woke up and took him for a walk. Santa Paws loved to sleep, but he loved to go for walks even more. And the earlier the walk, the earlier he got to have breakfast *after* the walk. Breakfast was one of Santa Paws' favorite times of day. It was right up there with dinner. And with treat

77

times, which came all through the day. You could never predict when somebody might give you a treat. But—why wasn't Patricia getting up?

Santa Paws stuck his nose under the covers and poked Patricia's arm.

"Hey!" she yelled. "That's one cold nose, buddy!" But his little nudge had done the trick. Patricia sighed again, threw off the covers, and climbed out of bed. Still in a bit of a daze, she splashed water on her face and combed her hair. She dressed quickly, clipped on Santa Paws' leash, and headed out to find Thomas.

"Whoa," she said, the moment she crested the low dunes between the hotel and the beach. "That is so uncool." The beach was a mess! Garbage and litter were strewn everywhere, up and down the beach, as far as Patricia could see.

Thomas stood in the middle of the beach, looking defeated. "Can you believe somebody did this?" he asked. "After all the work we put in yesterday."

Patricia shook her head. "It's awful!" she agreed. "This beach was cleaner than clean yesterday. Now look at it."

Santa Paws didn't know where to start. He liked helping with cleanup, but this was ridiculous. He couldn't take two steps without coming across a plastic bag, or a soda can, or a Styrofoam cup.

"Who would *do* this?" Patricia asked, stooping to pick up a potato-chip bag.

"I can guess."

Patricia glanced up to see that Thomas was looking in the direction of the lifeguard chair, which stood empty in the early-morning light. "Check this out," Thomas added, as he bent down to pick up a rumpled, sand-covered Santa hat. "Who do you think *this* belongs to?" He held it up for Patricia's inspection.

Patricia gasped. "Jax?" she asked. "He wouldn't really—" Then she remembered the way he had made fun of the environmental club. And Gregory had told her about the lifeguard's sneering surfer buddy, J-Dog or K-Dog or something. Maybe Jax *would* do something like this, just as a prank.

Thomas shrugged. "I'm not accusing anybody," he said. "The blame game is a total waste of time. Right now, I just want to get this all cleaned up." He held up two garbage bags. "What do you say?" he asked, pleadingly.

"But—" Patricia was about to point out that it was her *vacation*. She really did not want to spend another morning picking up trash. But Thomas looked like a cute puppy, begging for table scraps. How could she say no to those deep blue eyes? "What about the club?" she asked lamely.

Thomas shook his head. "I doubt they'd come out again so soon," he said. "People are so busy with Christmas shopping and all. I guess you are, too. That's okay."

He seemed so bummed out that Patricia felt she had no choice. "We all did our Christmas shopping before we left Oceanport. I guess I can help you," she said. Thomas's face lit up as she reached for a bag.

"Let's start at the other end of the beach this time," he suggested. "Race you!" He took off running.

Later on that morning, Emily and Mrs. Callahan headed out to check out their second Oasis pool. Mr. Callahan stayed behind "to keep the cats company," and work on his story. Gregory and Miranda headed onto the beach to meet up with Montana for the day's surfing lesson. And Steve, Lucy, and Cookie hit the beach, too, but this time Steve had plans for Lucy. He was going to keep her occupied, so she wouldn't wander off. He had noticed a flyer in the hotel lobby about a big sand castle contest to be held on Christmas Eve. He knew that Emily wouldn't want him to enter. "You're always so competitive," his wife would say. "You're on vacation. Forget entering the contest!"

But as soon as he had seen the poster, Steve had started thinking. He had Big Ideas about a castle that would knock any judge's socks off. Not that he was being competitive. Really, he just thought it would be an activity that he and Lucy could enjoy together.

"How about here?" he asked her now, setting down the big multi-colored beach umbrella he had brought from the hotel. He also dropped a cooler full of food and drinks, a beach blanket, and an armload of buckets, shovels, and trowels.

"No, Cookie wants to go over there!" Lucy said, pointing to a spot ten yards farther down the beach. The peppy black dog tugged on the leash Lucy held, nearly pulling the little girl over.

Steve sighed. "OK," he said, gathering everything up. "I had to ask!" he muttered to himself, as he lugged the supplies to the spot Cookie and Lucy had chosen. "This looks good," he agreed. "We're out of the way of the waves, but close enough to shore so that we have nice wet sand. Perfect for sand castles!"

"Perfect," echoed a sunburned man nearby. He was also with a small child, a boy about Lucy's age. "Are you entering the contest?" He and his son were working together on a sand castle. The boy filled buckets of sand and brought them to his father, who placed them carefully and patted them into firm towers.

Steve shrugged. "Today we're just building for fun. We'll see about the contest. How about you?"

The man shrugged, too. "Same here," he said. "I'm not really into competition."

"Right," said Steve. He didn't believe *that* for a minute. It only took one look at this guy's face, a study in concentration as he patted each tower into place, for Steve to tell he had met his match.

"That was great," Thomas was saying to Patricia, as they finished their cleanup. "I mean—the garbage part was a pain. But I liked talking to you while we picked it up! Thanks for helping. You're a trouper."

Patricia nodded tiredly. "You're welcome," she said. Two hours of garbage picking had worn her out. How could Thomas still be acting so happy and upbeat?

"So, what about swimming with the dolphins?" Thomas asked. "Want to try that this afternoon?"

Patricia shook her head. "I'm beat," she said. "All I want to do is lie by the pool. Maybe tomorrow?"

Thomas looked disappointed, but he managed an enthusiastic smile. "Sure!" he said. "That'd be great. Let's just hope the garbage vandal doesn't strike again."

Patricia held up crossed fingers. "Here's hoping!" she echoed, waving as Thomas loped off.

She watched him go. Then she walked over to the lifeguard chair and glared up at Jax. Her hands were on her hips, and she was frowning.

"Hey!" he said, smiling down at her.

Patricia didn't answer.

The smile vanished. "What is it?" he asked. "Don't tell me your cousin is missing again."

Patricia reached into her bag and pulled out the Santa hat. She'd taken it from Thomas just so she could confront Jax.

"Wow!" His face lit up. "Where did you find it? I've been looking all over for that hat."

"Oh, so it is yours," Patricia said, one eyebrow raised. "You admit it?"

"Admit it?" Jax asked, looking puzzled. "Sure!"

Patricia couldn't believe it. He wasn't even going to try to hide the fact that he was the beach vandal. She shook her head and tossed the hat up to him. "Here you go," she said. "Try to hang onto it this time."

"Uh—thanks!" said Jax.

Patricia was disgusted—and exhausted. She turned her back on Jax and trudged toward the hotel, with Santa Paws at her side.

She found her mother and her aunt lying contentedly by the Everglades pool. Trees dripping with Spanish moss and fiberglass flamingos and alligators placed here and there for effect surrounded this one.

Patricia flopped down next to her mother. "Ugh!" she said. "If I never see another piece of trash it'll be too soon." She told her mom and Emily all about how someone—"probably that lifeguard Jax"—had strewn garbage all over the beach.

"Terrible," said her aunt vaguely, barely looking up from her magazine.

"A real shame," said her mother. "But how can you be sure it was Jax?" She gestured to the mystery novel she was reading. "As the detective in this story says, 'things are rarely what they appear, and are often the opposite.'"

Patricia raised an eyebrow. "Interesting," she said thoughtfully. Then she lay down and fell happily asleep in the shade of a big green umbrella. Next to her, Santa Paws snoozed peacefully.

9

"Oh, Abigail, stop pacing," said Mr. Callahan. "You're ruining my concentration."

Abigail froze and looked up at him for a moment, her big green eyes wide open in an innocent, "who, me?" gaze. Then she resumed her activity. She wove her way around the couch and the low table, then stalked into the small ones' bedroom. Up onto the bed she leapt. She toyed for a moment with a stuffed gorilla, then jumped back down to the carpeted floor with a thump. Returning to the room where the man and Evelyn sat, she chased her tail around and around for a while, hoping Mr. Callahan would realize she was desperate for some *fun*. Then she stretched to her full length and began to sharpen her claws on the deliciously thick carpet.

"Abigail! No!" said Tom Callahan. He put down the *Florida Today* magazine he had been reading ("Research!" he would have insisted if any of his family members had caught him at it) and got up to stop for Abigail before she did any damage.

Too late—she sped off into the second bedroom, where she attacked the filmy curtains for a few moments before moving on to bat at the telephone cord.

Abigail was bored.

Sure, this house they were visiting was very comfy. She knew that Evelyn was satisfied lying around all day, with occasional breaks for eating the delicious treats that arrived after a knock at the door. But Evelyn was old and stodgy. Give her a cozy place to sleep, and she was content.

Not Abigail. Abigail had a feeling that there was more to this place than her people were letting her see. They came and went all day (well, except for this man, who mostly lay on the couch), and they brought new and enticing smells each time. Abigail wanted to see where those smells came from. Why was she a prisoner here? Why were they being so unfair? "Why, why, why?" she yowled.

Abigail wandered into the living room again, gave a disgusted look at the sleeping Evelyn, and stalked into the third bedroom. This was the room where the little ones' parents slept. She had heard them talking the night before. "Come on, Emily," the man had said. "I can't stand air-conditioning. It's not that hot out tonight. Can't we crack the window open instead?"

Now, Abigail discovered something very, very interesting. The outside smells were stronger in this room! She padded around the the room until she came to the window near the man's side of the bed. Abigail stood up on her hind feet to get a better look. Sure enough, the window was open. Abigail knew it would not pay to hesitate. Her boring days were at an end if she chose to take action. The time was now! Without a glance behind her, Abigail slipped outside.

Meanwhile, out on the beach, Cookie was also napping after a long morning of being chased by the waves, barking at them, and chasing them back out to sea. Lucy lay next to her on the blanket, dozing in the shade of the umbrella. But Steve was still hard at work on the castle. The father next to him also worked hard, while his son slept. Every time Steve added a wing onto his castle, the other man seemed to add two. And for every tower that the man built, Steve created three. Both sand castles already loomed over the men building them.

"Nice idea," the other man said to Steve during one of their trips with water-filled buckets. "I like the moat and drawbridge."

"Yours is great, too," said Steve. "Excellent towers. Where did you get the flags?" He looked enviously at the colorful pennants flying from the top of his neighbor's castle.

"Oh, those? I brought those from home," said the man. "Last year's contest winner had flags. The judges loved them."

Steve just nodded. Not competitive? Hah!

Down the beach, Gregory and Miranda were in the midst of their second surfing lesson. This time, Montana had herded the whole class right into the water. "No fooling around on shore today!" she had said. "You're all ready to catch some bigger waves."

All but me, Gregory thought, as he paddled his board out past the break. He just could not understand what the problem was. How could it be that all these little girls, including his cousin, were able to pop-up on their boards and ride wave after wave into shore—while he, Gregory, couldn't seem to get himself into a standing position, much less stay that way for more than a second? What a loser. It was the most frustrating experience he had ever had.

Fortunately, he had managed so far to hide his clumsiness from Montana. Whenever she looked his way, he made sure to be "helping" Miranda. That always seemed to make Montana flash her big, bright smile.

She was smiling at him now, as she caught up to him paddling. "You're so sweet with your cousin," she said. "Not many guys would be so unselfish. No wonder she thinks you're a hero."

Gregory wondered if she would be able to tell he was blushing. Probably not, he realized with relief. It would just look like a sunburn. "I'm not a hero," he said. "My *dog* is a hero, but not me."

Montana nodded back toward shore. "Was that your dog?" she asked.

Gregory knew what she meant. Earlier, they had seen Patricia with that hippie boy Thomas. They were each lugging a bulging plastic bag. Santa Paws had been loping along next to them, carrying something in his mouth. "Yup," he said. "That was Santa Paws."

"And the girl?" Montana asked. "Is that your girlfriend?"

Gregory was horrified. "No *way!*" he said. "That's my sister."

For a second, Gregory could have sworn that Montana looked relieved.

Out at the Everglades pool, Patricia woke with a start from her nap. Somewhere nearby, Santa Paws was barking his head off. "What is it?" she asked, looking around wildly.

"I can't imagine," said her mother, glancing up from her book. "Can't you make him be quiet? The other guests are going to complain."

"Mom, that's his 'danger' bark," Patricia said. Her mom's brains must be fried by the sun if she couldn't recognize that this bark meant trouble.

Patricia jumped up and looked around. Santa Paws was standing at full alert, his ears forward and his nose thrust toward a jungle area just beyond Emily's lounge chair. Patricia tiptoed over and peered into the underbrush.

"Oh. My. God." she said, backing away.

"What is it?" her mother asked. Eileen Callahan was realizing that something really *was* wrong.

"It's Abigail," Patricia said slowly.

"What? How did she get out?"

"I don't know," Patricia answered. "But she did. And now she's being stalked by an alligator."

Emily burst out laughing. "That's not a real alligator. It's just a stone replica!" she told her niece. "One of the garden ornaments. They *are* very realistic, aren't they?"

Patricia was still backing away. Her face was white. "It's not a replica," she said, shaking her head. "It's moving. And it's moving toward Abigail."

Abigail was crouching. Her fur was puffed up and her tail was lashing madly back and forth. She was staring at the horrible thing. Its eyes were as cold as ice, and its slithery tail slid from side to side as it crawled toward her on its scaly, short legs. She knew she had to run, run, run! But those cold eyes were holding her like magnets. Abigail couldn't seem to take even one step away from them. Why, oh why, had she ever thought she was bored? Now she wished more than anything to be back in that room with Evelyn. She would never explore again! Never!

Santa Paws barked louder. He had never seen anything like this creature, but he knew that it was evil and that it would not hesitate to gulp his cat friend Abigail as soon as it got close enough. What could he do? The creature's mouth was huge, and its teeth looked sharper than any the dog had ever seen. Santa Paws lunged toward the creature, hoping to scare it off. But the creature just kept lumbering toward Abigail, its yellow eyes fixed on the small black cat.

Santa Paws lunged again and again. "No, Santa Paws!" cried Patricia. What if the alligator turned on the dog? One bite from those huge jaws and Santa Paws would be history.

Then she heard men's voices behind her. "That dog must have him cornered!" someone yelled. "Bring the stun gun!" Three men raced through the pool area. When they spotted the alligator, one of them aimed a pistol.

Patricia covered her eyes.

"It's just a stun gun," one of the other men told her, "It shoots a chemical that will make Sultan drowsy, so we can capture him."

"Sultan?" Patricia asked. She was startled. The alligator had a name?

The man nodded. "He's a star attraction, over

at Smithie's Alligator Farm. He's also a regular escapee. Sultan is a real character. You should come pay him a visit!"

By now, the alligator had stopped moving. His head drooped to the ground and his awful tail went limp. Nap time.

Abigail had zipped into the bushes when the stun gun went off. Patricia got down on her hands and knees and pulled her out. "You're a bad girl," she scolded Abigail, holding the frightened cat closely and kissing her head. Then she reached down and patted Santa Paws. "And you are a good, good boy." Abigail started to purr. All was well now. She was safe.

That night, the Callahans headed down to Manatee Beach for the Sunset Celebration, a kind of fair held every night. People came from all over the island. "There'll be jugglers, and fire-eaters, and live music," Mr. Callahan said. "Just the kind of event vacationers will want to hear about."

It was also just the kind of event Patricia loved. But she didn't go along. She wanted to be on the hotel beach that night. Alone. Except for Santa Paws, of course. No detective does a stakeout without a sidekick along. And that's what Patricia was planning to be: a detective.

Somebody was messing up the beach. And Patricia was determined to find out who. She had assumed that it was Jax—but ever since her mother read that comment about things seldom being what they seem, Patricia had begun to wonder.

Just after sunset, the sky was deep blue and the beach was quiet and magical under the light of a rising full moon. The only sound was the gentle lapping of waves on the shore. Patricia and Santa Paws crouched behind a red-striped cabana, waiting and watching. Would the vandal appear again tonight? Patricia wasn't sure whether to hope that he (or she?) would—or wouldn't. If the vandal made another mess, it might mean she would have to help clean up the beach *again*. On the other hand, if no vandal showed up, she'd never know who it was.

At first, Patricia's heart was beating fast. But soon, she began to realize what every detective probably knows all too well: Stakeouts are boring. So boring, in fact, that it's not always easy for even the most dedicated detective to stay awake.

Patricia dozed off, leaning against the warm bulk of Santa Paws. But she was jolted awake a few minutes later, when her dog sprang to attention. "Oh! What is it?" she whispered. "Is someone there?"

Santa Paws gave a low whimper. Patricia peered around the corner of the cabana.

Sure enough, a dark figure was slipping through the shadows cast by the next cabana. Who was it?

Patricia squinted, but she couldn't tell. Was it the beach vandal?

No. Now there was *another* figure approaching the beach. A figure with a strange, lumpy shape. Humpback? No, Patricia realized. A boy.

A boy carrying a bulging bag of garbage.

10

"**I** can't believe you're spending your day off on this!" It was the next morning, bright and early—though not *quite* as early as the previous two mornings, thankfully. The sun shone down, the sky was blue, and Florida was a beautiful place to be. Patricia smiled over at the boy at the wheel of the bright red convertible she was riding in.

"Why not?" he asked. "You said it was always a dream of yours to swim with the dolphins, didn't you? Well, now that you're here in Florida, it's time to make that dream come true." He took his eyes off the road for a moment to look at her and grin his crooked grin.

"You're really sweet, Jax," said Patricia. She swallowed the hard lump of guilt that was doing its best to ruin her day. How could Jax ever know that she had suspected him of being the beach vandal? It wasn't as if she'd accused him outright, after all. Still, she felt terrible. Not only was he

95

not the guilty party, but he had been so upset by the vandalism that he, too, had staked out the beach the night before.

So it had ended up being the two of them, Jax and Patricia (plus Santa Paws, of course) who had caught Thomas.

Yes, Thomas. The boy with the garbage bag—the beach vandal, caught red-handed!—had turned out to be none other than Patricia's cute, sweet, environmentalist.

And the other shadowy figure, behind the cabana? Jax.

Jax had come out in hopes of catching the person who had messed up the beach. It turned out that he felt very, very strongly about clean beaches. He even belonged to a group called Surfers Against Sewage.

"Hey, dude," Jax had said to Thomas, shining his flashlight into Thomas's startled face while Santa Paws sniffed at the garbage bag. "I thought you were, like, Mr. I Love The Environment Guy."

"I am!" said Thomas. Even in the weak beam of the flashlight, Patricia could tell he was blushing.

"So what's the 411 on this, then?" Jax asked, gesturing toward the bag.

Thomas's shoulders slumped. "It's hard to explain."

"Give it a try," Jax prompted.

Thomas shot a look at Patricia, and his blush

deepened. "It was just that I wanted to . . ." his voice trailed off into a mumble as he turned his face away from the circle of light.

"Wanted to *what?*" Patricia asked. She honestly had not understood him. She reached down to pull Santa Paws away from the garbage he was sniffing.

Thomas sighed a long, low sigh. "I wanted to spend more time with you," he blurted out.

Patricia stared at him. She could hardly believe her ears. "You *what?*"

"Don't make me say it again," Thomas begged. "I know it was a jerky thing to do." He hung his head and kicked at the sand. "I just — I really liked being with you the other morning. And I wanted to make sure we had more time together."

Patricia shook her head. "I don't believe it," she said.

"Dude," Jax said, "ever hear of asking someone on a date?"

"I know, I know," Thomas said. "What can I say? I'm a dope."

Patricia softened. "No, you're not," she said. "Not at all. You're a great guy — who did a dopey thing."

Santa Paws seemed to sense how upset Thomas was. He stuck his nose into the boy's hand. "Hey, Santa Paws," Thomas said miserably. Then he picked up the garbage bag and hoisted it over his shoulder. "Guess I better go find a Dumpster to toss this into," he said. "Are you—are you going to tell anybody else?"

"No worries, dude," Jax said.

"Just don't do it again, OK?" Patricia asked.

"I swear," Thomas said. And he took off, leaving Patricia and Jax alone (that is, except for Santa Paws) on the beach.

Patricia shook her head. "Wild!" she said. "I can't believe he did that just to spend time with me!"

Jax took her hand. "I can," he said. "Come on. It's a beautiful night. Let's go for a walk."

They walked and talked until Patricia suddenly realized that her family must be wondering where she was. That was when Jax had learned about her wish to swim with the dolphins, and had immediately suggested that they go the next day. He had even said she could ask Gregory, Miranda, and Lucy along. But Gregory and Miranda had wanted to surf. They had heard that a big storm was working its way toward Florida, and this might be their last day to try out their new skills. And Lucy had insisted on helping her dad build another sand castle to practice for the contest on Christmas Eve.

Now, fifteen minutes after they had left The Oasis, Jax pulled his convertible into a parking lot near a long, low building that sprawled along the beach front. "This is the best place to meet dolphins," he told Patricia. "It's not a tourist trap. It's a real research facility. The people here know everything there is to know about dolphins. They care for a few injured ones here, and they swim with them every day! My cousin works here, and she told me I was welcome anytime."

Patricia's heart was beating fast as she followed Jax around the back of the building to where the dolphins lived, in a huge pen in the ocean that kept them safe.

"Oh!" she said, as they rounded the corner. Just at that moment, a dolphin was leaping high out of the water to take a fish held out by a young woman. The dolphin's sleek gray body glistened in the sun as it burst from the water and grabbed the fish in one graceful movement. As the dolphin fell back with a splash, the woman turned and saw them. A smile spread across her face. "Hey, cuz!" she said. She pulled another fish from her bucket and dangled it high. "Here for breakfast?"

Back at The Oasis, Eileen and Emily Callahan had just settled in at their third pool. "This is awesome," Emily said, looking around. "I think this one might be my favorite."

The Jungle pool was landscaped with thick, flowering vines and huge tropical plants. A large net cage held brightly-colored parrots. A skinny brown monkey scampered around freely inside the cage, swinging from vine to vine. There was even a small replica of an Aztec temple, looking like an ancient ruin found in the deep jungle.

"Lovely," Eileen agreed, leaning back with a sigh. "This is the most restful Christmas I've ever had." Above her, a palm-frond umbrella waved slightly in the breeze. She reached into her tote bag to pull out her book. "Maybe I'll finish this one today," she said happily.

"There you are!" Suddenly, Mr. Callahan emerged from behind a purple-flowered plant. "I've been looking all over for you."

Eileen looked at him over her sunglasses. "You have?" she asked suspiciously. "Why?" She was surprised to see her husband out and about, even in the cooler part of the day.

He rubbed his hands together happily. "You're going to love this," he said. "I've booked you on a banana boat ride!"

"A what?" asked Emily. "And—why?"

Tom grinned. "A banana boat is a long, yellow inflatable raft that gets towed behind a speed-boat, like a water ski. You sit astride it and go for the ride of your life!"

Eileen looked unimpressed. "OK, that's the 'what,'" she said. "How about the 'why'? Why on earth would we want to do something like that?"

"Because it'll be fun!" Tom said, working hard to keep the enthusiasm in his voice. "And . . . because it'll give me something to write about."

"Aha!" said Emily. "I *knew* there was a reason. If you want to write about it, why don't *you* do it?"

Tom looked shocked. "Are you kidding?" he said. "No way! I'd have to be crazy to—I mean, I want to be able to retain my journalistic objectivity is what I mean."

"Right," said his wife drily. She leaned back in her chair. "I don't think so."

Tom's face fell. "Please?" he begged. "As a favor to me? Please?"

Eileen looked at Emily. "What do you think?" she asked. "I suppose it could actually be fun."

Emily looked at Eileen. "And I suppose we should do at least one wild thing on our Florida vacation."

"Exactly!" crowed Tom. "That's excellent!" He checked his watch. "You're due on the beach in half an hour."

Gregory, Miranda, Steve, and Lucy stared in disbelief as Eileen and Emily straddled the long banana-shaped inflatable raft and took hold of handles that stuck up along the top. Cookie whimpered, and Santa Paws looked concerned. "Are you sure that thing is safe?" Steve asked Tom.

"You bet!" Tom said. "They run this thing all the time."

Tom didn't mention to his brother that the speedboat driver who would be towing the banana boat, a Santa-hatted Texan named Bud, had just asked the two women to sign a long document that promised they wouldn't sue anybody if they got hurt.

"You gals don't have to worry about a thang!" hollered Bud, as he bent over the motor on his speedboat. It started up with a roar.

"Isn't anybody else riding with us?" Emily yelled to him. There were at least six other spots on the raft.

"Nope, just you two, today!" Bud yelled back. "Hang on, now!" He whooped as he opened up the throttle and the boat leapt forward, jerking the raft behind it through the choppy waves.

Bang! Bang! Bang! The raft hit each wave hard, and it was all Eileen and Emily could do to hang on. Then Bud turned the wheel of the speedboat, and the yellow raft leaned hard to the right, almost throwing them off as they slid sideways, holding onto the handles for dear life.

"Is this supposed to be fun?" Emily yelled to her sister-in-law.

"I'm going to kill him!" was all Eileen answered in return.

Bud glanced back with a huge grin, "Yee-haw!" he yelled, waving his Santa hat in the air.

"Slow down!" Emily shouted back. She gestured with one hand, holding on desperately with the other.

Unfortunately, Bud seemed to think her gesture meant, "speed up!" He revved the boat and made three more huge circles, each one faster than the last. The under-weighted raft bounced high each time it hit a wave, and leaned way over every time it followed the speedboat's arc on a sweeping turn.

"I — think — I'm — going — to — be — sick!" Emily called out, as the pounding continued.

"I don't know how much longer I can hang on!" Eileen yelled back.

Finally, Bud seemed to realize that they weren't exactly having the time of their lives. With a shrug, he slowed down and headed toward shore. Then, something seemed to get the better of him, and he sped up and made one more wide, sweeping turn.

"Whoa!" Emily yelled, as she slipped off the banana boat. "Help!" Then she hit the water hard. "Ouch!"

Eileen couldn't do a thing to help her sister-in-law. She was still holding on for dear life as the speedboat raced toward shore. *Tom is going to pay for this*, she thought.

Back on the beach, Santa Paws and Cookie both heard Emily's voice. Without hesitation, they plunged into the waves and swam steadily out, making a beeline for the terrified woman.

"Oh, oh, it hurts!" she cried, as she thrashed

around, trying to keep her head above water. "I can't breathe!" A searing pain rushed through her chest as she gasped in fear.

Then, she felt herself supported on both sides as Santa Paws and Cookie reached her and nudged her toward the surface. She managed to throw one arm around Santa Paws' neck and grab onto Cookie's collar with the other hand.

Slowly, steadily, the two dogs towed Emily back to shore.

11

"And then Laverne let me hold onto her fin and she towed me all over the pen! Oh, and then Shirley kissed me!" Patricia's words were tumbling out in her excitement. She was still glowing from her day with the dolphins, and she wanted to tell her family every detail. "Did I mention that bottlenose dolphins are actually small whales? And that they breathe through a blowhole?"

"I believe you mentioned that, yes," said her father.

"Like, approximately a billion times already," Gregory added. He reached for another french fry. The Callahans were settled in for the evening, having a room-service dinner of burgers and fries. Santa Paws was on the newspaper-covered carpet near Gregory's feet, gnawing on a huge soup bone that the kitchen had sent along, while Cookie, next to Miranda, nibbled daintily on a peanut-butter cookie. Abigail and Evelyn were stretched

105

out on the couch. They had already scarfed down the fish scraps the kitchen had sent for them.

"And yes, you also already mentioned that they hang out in groups called pods, and that they can live to be twenty-five years old —" Gregory went on, before Patricia could continue her lecture.

"And that Stanley knows how to shake hands, or rather, fins," Miranda interrupted, getting in on the act.

"Now, come on, you two," said Mr. Callahan. "Patricia's just excited about her day, that's all. I, for one, am very pleased to learn some things I didn't know about dolphins."

"So am I," agreed Steve. "Very interesting." But then, Patricia noticed, he immediately changed the subject. "Lucy and I are all ready for the sand castle contest tomorrow. You should see the model we made today. It is *spectacular.* In fact, I think we have a really good chance of winning."

Emily cleared her throat. "Can you say, 'competitive'?" she asked. She let out a short laugh, then winced. "Ow, that hurts," she said, holding her side. Emily was lying on the couch with the cats. Beside her was the most humongous bunch of flowers any of them had ever seen. *So sorry about your broken rib!* read the card from Big Jim Jessup, who had somehow heard about her accident.

Tom Callahan looked concerned. "How long

did the doctor say it would take to heal?" He obviously felt somewhat responsible for Emily's injury.

"About three weeks," said Emily. "Not that I'll have to stay in bed the whole time." She smiled at her husband. "In fact," she went on, "I fully intend to get myself onto the beach tomorrow morning to watch you and Lucy build your prize-winning sand castle."

"If there *is* a contest," Gregory said. "You know, we're supposed to be getting a big storm." He had been hearing about this all day from Montana. The coming storm, according to her, was going to create gigantic waves and some of the best surfing conditions of the winter. Not that Gregory would be out there on those killer waves. He knew he just didn't have what it took to ride a wave twenty feet tall. Not yet, anyway. Someday, maybe. He had already decided to save up for a wetsuit and practice his surfing in the frigid Rhode Island waters. If the Callahans ever came back to Christmas Island, he'd show Montana what he could do.

"Montana says the waves are going to be awesome," Miranda said. "She says there's nothing like surfing the big ones."

"Montana says, Montana says." Patricia rolled her eyes. "That's all you ever talk about anymore!"

"Hey!" Miranda looked hurt.

"I'm sorry," Patricia said quickly. "I know you like Montana. And she definitely knows a lot about surfing." Patricia had to admit it to herself: Maybe she was just a teeny bit jealous that her cousin had found another role model, an older girl she could look up to. Still, that was no reason to dislike Montana.

"Anyway," Mrs. Callahan said. "I don't think any of us will be on the beach tomorrow. The weather forecast is really bad: wind, rain, thunderstorms, and who knows what else. And to think it will be Christmas Eve."

"Do you think they'll have to cancel the boat parade?" Emily asked. She and the rest of the Callahans had been looking forward to the Christmas Day boat parade, which was a big tradition on Christmas Island. Everybody who had a boat loaded it up with Christmas lights, and then at dusk on Christmas the whole flotilla would make its way up the coast, while spectators applauded from the shore. There would be music, and lots of Santas, and candy and cookies and hot chocolate. There was even a rumor that Big Jim Jessup might make an appearance at The Oasis.

Mr. Callahan was shrugging. "Depends on how long it takes for the storm to blow itself out, I guess," he said. "I sure hope the parade still happens. It'll make a great centerpiece for my story." He scratched his head. "Now, if I could only find a good opening," he said.

"Don't look at me!" said his wife. "No more banana boats for this woman. I've had enough adventures on this trip, and I'm spending the rest of my vacation by the pool. Even if it's only the indoor pool because of the weather."

"I'm with Eileen," Emily told her brother-in-law. "Have your own adventures if you want something to write about, and quit using us as guinea pigs!" She delivered this with a big smile, to show that there were no hard feelings.

Santa Paws looked up from his bone and woofed, as if in agreement. Cookie chimed in, with her higher-pitched bark.

Mr. Callahan held up his hands. "OK, OK," he said. "I get the message."

That night, Gregory could hear the wind picking up outside as he lay in bed, trying to sleep. The weather seemed to make Santa Paws nervous: He paced in and out of Gregory's bedroom as if he couldn't find a place to settle down.

By the time dawn broke, the windows in Gregory's room were rattling as high winds battered the hotel. Gregory was almost happy to hear that the storm was so wild. At least now Montana would have the sense to stay inside. Nobody in their right mind would surf on a day like this! He rolled over to snooze for a few more minutes, knowing that he would have to get up soon and take Santa Paws outside, no matter how horrible the weather was. Unless Patricia got up first, of course.

Unfortunately, she didn't. Patricia could sleep through anything.

When Santa Paws stuck his cold nose into Gregory's hand for the third time, Gregory finally heaved himself out of bed. "OK, OK," he said, yawning as he pulled on his jeans and sweatshirt. "Here we go."

He led Santa Paws out into the hall, but they hadn't even gotten to the exit when Gregory heard someone calling his name.

"Geggy! Geggy! Wait for me!"

It was Lucy. What was she doing up so early? "Hey, punkin," Gregory said, bending down to pick up his cousin. "What are you up to?"

"Looking for 'Randa," Lucy said, staring up at him with serious eyes.

"Miranda?" Gregory asked. "Isn't she in your room?"

Lucy shook her head.

"Maybe she's playing hide-and-seek," Gregory said. He looked down at Santa Paws. "You're going to have to be patient, big guy," he said. He walked Lucy back down the hall and into the suite she shared with her parents, and aunt and uncle. Gregory looked around the living room area. "Hello?" he said softly. "Miranda?"

Evelyn came over and twined herself around Gregory's ankles. Abigail gave one of her "feed me!" meows. But Miranda didn't stick her head up from behind the couch, as Gregory had expected her to.

After he'd checked the girls' room, Gregory knocked on Emily and Steve's door. "Uncle Steve? Aunt Emily?"

In a moment, Steve opened the door, yawning as he scratched his head. "Hey, Gregory. What's up?" He looked bewildered.

"Is Miranda with you?" Gregory asked.

"Nope," Steve said. "She and Lucy have been sleeping in their own room. They usually don't even wake us up until eight or so."

"What's going on?" asked Eileen Callahan, coming out of the other room.

"We're looking for Miranda. She's not in your room, is she?" Steve asked.

Gregory saw his aunt's eyes grow big as his mother shook her head. He was starting to get a bad feeling in his stomach.

Santa Paws felt it, too. Something was wrong. There was a familiar prickling along his spine. He began to pant and pace and whine.

"Wait," Gregory said to his uncle. "What about Cookie? Where is she?"

Steve's eyes met Gregory's. "Oh, no," he said. "They're both missing?"

Just then, Santa Paws pricked up his ears. It was hard to hear anything over the howling of the wind, but wasn't that—? He cocked his head this way and that. Yes! Suddenly, he was sure. He could hear the sound of Cookie barking from far out on the beach. She needed his help. She needed it *now*!

Santa Paws pulled hard on the leash Gregory was holding. No more patience. No more waiting. It was time to go.

Gregory and Santa Paws ran for the exit. When Gregory opened the door, the wind slammed it open against the outer wall. "Whoa!" said Gregory, when he felt its full blast against his face. Driving rain pelted him as he bent his head and forged forward, leaning into the wind as Santa Paws towed him toward the beach.

Suddenly, Gregory realized exactly where it was Miranda must have gone. She had slipped out to look for her hero, Montana! Miranda thought the surfers were going to be out in the big waves. She wanted to watch. "Oh, no," Gregory groaned. He ran even faster, slipping and sliding in the wet sand as he crested the dunes.

He gasped when he saw the waves. They were immense, bigger than he had ever imagined. They rolled toward the shore like towering walls of water, dwarfing the lifeguard stand that stood rocking in the wind.

"Miranda!" Gregory yelled, but the wind snatched the word right out of his mouth. She wouldn't have heard him even if she were standing two feet away.

But Santa Paws heard something. Gregory could tell by the way he was standing at attention, both ears turned toward the roaring surf.

"What is it, Big Guy?" Gregory asked.

Santa Paws pulled hard on the leash. Gregory bent to unclip it. He knew that his dog had a job to do. Gregory hated to let Santa Paws loose to run into the heart of this wild storm. But Santa Paws could take care of himself. He always had before! Gregory gave Santa Paws a quick hug. "Be careful," he said, in a voice choked with fear. "Be careful, Big Guy."

Gregory swallowed hard as he watched his dog tear off into the driving wind and rain. Then he started to run after him.

Santa Paws felt no hesitation. Even though he couldn't see much through his rain-stung eyes, he could hear Cookie's bark as clear as a bell. He charged faster, faster, feeling the sand fly up beneath his paws as he galloped toward the shoreline.

There she was! Cookie stood at the edge of the ocean, barking into the dark, crashing waves. Santa Paws ran up to her and the two dogs briefly touched noses. Then Santa Paws turned to look into the surf.

Gregory raced toward the dogs, peering into the surf as he ran. He could just make out some figures in the distance: three of them, riding surfboards toward shore on a huge, gray wall of water. Montana! Gregory thought, when he caught a glimpse of white-blond hair. And then, he saw a fourth figure, a small one, at the edge of the water. That figure began to move closer to the waves, as if pulled by the sight of the surfers.

"Miranda!" Gregory screamed, when he recognized his cousin. "Stop!" But it was too late. Gregory watched in horror as a huge wave crashed down on his cousin and swept her out to sea.

Then, just as Gregory caught up with Santa Paws, one of the surfboards flipped up, dumping its passenger into the breaking, surging surf. "Oh, no!" Gregory shouted. "Montana!" He grabbed his dog's collar as Santa Paws rushed into the water, "I'm coming with you, Big Guy!" he said. Gregory, Santa Paws, and Cookie forged their way into the raging surf.

With Gregory holding on and kicking to help propel their way through the waves, Santa Paws swam hard, harder than he had ever swum before. Next to him, Cookie's legs churned through the roiling water. In moments, they had caught up to Miranda. She looked at them helplessly as waves tossed her small body this way and that. "Miranda!" Gregory yelled. "Grab Cookie's collar! She'll tow you back to land!"

Miranda stared at him with frightened eyes, her arms flailing around for balance as the waves did their best to sweep her farther out to sea.

"Just do it!" Gregory yelled. Salt water slapped

his face and choked off his words, but Miranda obeyed, grabbing her dog's collar. "I'm going out with Santa Paws!" He hung tightly to his dog's collar as Santa Paws kept paddling through the heavy waves.

At first, Gregory thought they would *never* find Montana. He couldn't see anything but water. Water surrounded him. It bashed his body and filled his mouth and blurred his vision.

But Santa Paws seemed to know exactly where he was going. He swam with a strength Gregory had never seen before, motoring through the churning water like a steamboat. And then, suddenly, there was Montana, holding desperately onto her surfboard as she bobbed in the waves. "Help!" she cried. "Help me!"

"Take his collar," Gregory instructed, panting. "He'll tow you. I'll pull your board in."

"What about the other guys?" Montana whirled around, trying to see her friends. "What about Jax and G-Dog?"

"Just grab on!" Gregory shouted. Right now he could only think about saving Montana. As far as he knew, the boys had ridden their surfboards all the way to the beach. "They're fine!" he said, hoping she would believe him.

When Gregory, Montana, and Santa Paws finally dragged themselves out of the surf, they found all the Callahans waiting for them. Tom was there, along with Eileen and Steve, who was holding a frightened, wailing Lucy in his arms. Cookie was standing, exhausted, at the edge of the surf, as Emily rubbed Miranda with a towel, trying to calm her crying. Eileen and Tom Callahan rushed toward their son. "Gregory!" his mother cried, sobbing as she pulled him into her arms.

Gregory let himself sink into the hug, but only for a second. Then he stepped back. "What about the others?" he asked urgently. "What about Jax and G-Dog? Did they make it?"

"Look!" Patricia pointed down the beach. "What's that?"

Far off in the distance, a pair of figures staggered out of the waves and collapsed onto shore.

"It's them!" Gregory said. "Jax and G-dog! Everybody's safe!"

But everybody *wasn't* safe. "No! Cookie!" Miranda shrieked. A huge wave had just crashed over the little black dog. Before anyone could move, the wave swept Cookie far out, into the choppy gray sea.

Santa Paws, soaked and trembling with exhaustion, did not hesitate. He plunged into the waves after his friend. There was no stopping him. He would save her, or die trying.

Gregory watched helplessly as Santa Paws forged his way through the roiling gray sea. Then he turned toward Patricia. When their eyes met, sister and brother shared an unspoken fear.

This time, the dogs might not come back.

12

Santa Paws choked and coughed as the stinging, salty water flooded his nose. His legs were so tired, and his whole body felt battered. As his strength ebbed away, it was becoming harder and harder to fight the waves. Every cell in his body screamed for rest. It would be so easy to let the waves carry him back to shore, back to Gregory and Patricia. But where was his friend? Where was Cookie? She needed his help. She needed him as nobody else had needed him before.

He swam and swam, his legs moving automatically as he fought to keep his nose above the churning water. Cookie's cries were becoming more and more distant, and he couldn't seem to catch even a glimpse of her.

For the first time in his life, Santa Paws felt like giving up. The angry sea had gotten the better of him. He felt weak, and tired, and . . . old.

If he could only rest for just a moment. If he could only catch his breath.

Santa Paws let his legs stop churning. He closed his eyes as his head dipped below the surface of the water. And he waited for whatever came next.

And then something incredible happened. Something amazing.

Santa Paws felt a bump against his rib cage, and then another. *Bump. Bump.* He was being pushed back up, up toward the surface. He stuck his nose above water and took a deep, desperate breath. He coughed, and breathed again. The air filled his lungs and he suddenly knew that he would be all right. After all the years of saving others, Santa Paws was now the one who needed to be saved. And some creature had sensed that. Some creature had come to his rescue.

A glimpse of its strong, slick gray back and long pointed nose told the dog that the creature was one he had never met before. This creature was at home in the sea, even when the sea was this wild. It moved without effort, carrying Santa Paws along as easily as it swam. Instead of fighting the waves, as Santa Paws had, it seemed to dance with them, the way Santa Paws danced with Gregory.

Santa Paws knew he was safe now. But what about Cookie? What about his friend? Again, he glanced wildly around, hoping to spot her curly dark head above the waves. And—yes! There she was, not far away. She, too, was supported by one of the sleek gray creatures.

Cookie was safe. Santa Paws relaxed and let himself be carried along. Over the roar of wind and water he heard the two creatures chatter to each other with a high-pitched clicking noise. It was a sound unlike any he had ever heard before, but somehow he knew it was language. Still, no matter how hard he strained to understand, he could not make out its meaning.

How long did this ride go on? Santa Paws had no sense of time. He only knew the bashing waves, the pounding rain, the shrieking wind. Then, finally, he felt solid earth beneath his feet! As he found his footing, he felt the creature slip away.

Now Cookie was by his side. Tiredly, they touched noses, then turned to watch their rescuers dive back into the gray, roiling depths. Santa Paws barked a grateful farewell. Then he and Cookie hauled themselves up onto shore.

But—where was Gregory? Where was Patricia? Santa Paws looked up and down the beach, but there was not a person in sight. Wherever he and Cookie were, it was far, far away from the people who loved them best. How would they ever find their people?

Santa Paws was much too tired to figure that out. And as for Cookie, she had collapsed on the sand as soon as she had gotten clear of the waves.

Exhausted, Santa Paws curled up next to her and fell instantly asleep.

Both dogs slept hard and long. In fact, they slept the day away. When Santa Paws woke up, the wind had died down, the rain had slowed, and the sky had already begun to darken.

Groggily, he looked around. What had woken him? Santa Paws had been dreaming about Gregory giving him a whole box of Milk-Bones, but as soon as he woke up he knew that Gregory was nowhere nearby. Still, something had startled him awake. Cookie, too. She had leapt to her feet. Her ears were pricked up, and she was staring into the gathering dusk.

Santa Paws turned to find out what Cookie was looking at.

The sight made the fur on the back of his neck stand straight up. What was *this*?

Eight or nine huge animals, like the deer he had once seen in the woods near home, stamped their feet in the sand. There was the sound of jingling bells when they shook their antlered heads. They were attached, to one another and to a huge red sleigh, with long leather lines that were knotted and tangled. The sleigh lay on its side in the sand, one runner buried and the other tilted up toward the sky. Toys and brightly colored boxes tied with beautiful ribbons lay scattered for yards around.

And sitting in the middle of it all was a large,

round man in a fur-trimmed red suit, black boots, and a very familiar-looking hat. The man had a long, white beard and flowing white hair. He was bent over, his face in his hands, and he did not seem to see the dogs.

Usually, when Santa Paws saw something new and strange, he barked at it. That always seemed like a good idea. When you barked at something, you could see how it reacted. Sometimes, the thing ran away. Then you didn't have to worry about it anymore. Sometimes, it became clear that the thing was a friend. Then you could stop barking and start asking for pats and treats.

This time, though, Santa Paws did not feel like barking. Cookie didn't bark, either. Instead, both dogs walked stiffly over to the man and sat down at his feet. Santa Paws lifted one paw and gently tapped the man's shoulder.

"What? Oh! You startled me!" the man said, looking up at Santa Paws and Cookie. Suddenly, he smiled. "Well, look at you two. Aren't you a pair?"

Santa Paws cocked his head. Something about the man's smile made Santa Paws feel warm all over, and he forgot right away how sore and achy his tired muscles felt.

The man reached out to pat each dog in turn. "Where did you two come from?" he asked. Then, as if to himself, he continued, "I suppose you were right here when I crashed. I just didn't see you.

I was too busy worrying about my reindeer, and the presents, and how I'm going to get everything done tonight." He shook his head. "This is not a good situation. I can't even get my sleigh upright. Not by myself, I can't. From now on I'm going to bring an elf or two along, just in case."

Santa Paws stood up. He could tell that this man needed help.

"Look at you," the man said. "You look awfully big and strong. I wonder . . ." He stroked his beard. "Think you could help me, big guy?"

When Santa Paws heard that nickname, the one that Gregory always called him, he forgot his sore muscles and his worries about finding his way home. He stood up straighter. His eyes brightened, and his ears pricked to attention. Help? Of course he could help!

"Ho, ho, ho." The man laughed. "Why, it's almost as if you understood me! How about your sidekick, there? Can the little one help, too?"

When she saw the man look her way, Cookie jumped to her feet.

"She looks clever," the man said. "Perhaps she could untangle these reins so my reindeer can fly again."

Cookie understood. It was like when her leash was tangled. She grabbed hold of the leather strap and shook her head, working out the knots.

Meanwhile, the man and Santa Paws stood looking at the tilted sleigh. "Maybe if we both push with all our strength . . ." the man said. He bent to put a shoulder against the sleigh's side. Santa Paws joined him, pushing the bulk of his body into the job.

"And a-one, and a-two, and a-HEAVE!" shouted the man. The sleigh rocked side to side and then, finally, flopped over onto its runners.

"Wonderful!" the man said, holding his big belly as he laughed heartily. "Look at that. Who needs a tow truck when you have a buddy to help push you out?"

Cookie stepped back from her work and barked, spinning around three times in a circle.

"And you fixed the reins!" the jolly man cried. "My goodness, what good helpers I have." He looked around at all the toys and presents spilled on the ground. "Now, there's just one more thing to do," he said. He bent and began to pick the packages up, stuffing each one into a huge bag on the back of the sleigh.

It was like a game. Santa Paws and Cookie ran to and fro, picking up every parcel they could hold in their teeth and carrying it back to the sleigh. They dropped them in the sand in a big pile, and the man loaded them onto the sleigh. Soon the bag was bulging and the beach was clear again.

By then, the reindeer were stamping their feet impatiently. Their harnesses jingled as they shook their heads and pawed at the ground.

"Yes, yes, my dears," said the man. "You're

ready to be off, aren't you?" The man checked all the harnesses and examined the sleigh carefully. "I think our pre-flight check shows that we're ready to go!" he said finally.

Santa Paws and Cookie sat on the sand, watching their friend with alert eyes. Maybe this man could tell them how to find their family!

As if he were reading their minds, he said, "I'll be happy to help you get you back to your loved ones. But first, would you like to go for a ride with me? It'll be the adventure of a lifetime, I promise you that!"

Go for a ride! Both dogs knew what *that* meant. They loved going for rides. First Santa Paws, and then Cookie, leapt into the sleigh and nestled in next to the man. He grabbed the reins and shook them, making the bells jingle happily.

"Ho, ho, ho!" he cried again. "What do you say, Donner? Ready to go, Blitzen? Rudolph, will you light our way?"

And with that, the reindeer moved forward—and upward! The huge sleigh rose into the sky behind the graceful bodies of the reindeer, soaring over the beach and the now-quiet sea like a big, red comet.

13

"**H**ey."
       "Hey."

Patricia and Gregory faced each other across the living room of their suite. They had both just emerged from their bedrooms, sleepy and yawning. The morning sun shone brightly through the windows, the sky was blue, and the fronds on the palm trees outside were completely still: Not so much as a breeze remained from yesterday's storm.

It was Christmas Day. The worst Christmas ever, as far as Gregory was concerned. He looked at Patricia's tired, wan face and knew that she would agree. With Santa Paws and Cookie still missing, how could they possibly feel otherwise?

"Merry Christmas, I guess," Gregory muttered.

"Yup," Patricia said.

"Sleep any?" he asked.

She shook her head. "Not really. You?"

He shrugged. "Nope."

Patricia went to the door and opened it, not even daring to hope that Santa Paws might be waiting outside. He wasn't, of course. The hallway was empty.

Gregory stood at the window, looking out at the beautiful morning. What good were sunshine and blue skies—without Santa Paws to share them with? Suddenly, Gregory *hated* Florida and everything about it. Stupid palm trees. Dumb old sun. He wanted to be back home in Rhode Island, waking up to a normal Christmas. What did palm trees have to do with Christmas, anyway?

The phone rang, and Patricia and Gregory both dove for it. Patricia grabbed it first. "Hello?" she said hopefully. Gregory crossed his fingers. Maybe someone had found the dogs!

"OK," Patricia said tonelessly. "We'll be there soon." She hung up. "That was Dad. We're supposed to head over to their suite for breakfast."

Gregory didn't even ask if there was any news about Santa Paws and Cookie. He didn't have to. It was obvious that there wasn't. "Right, let's go," he said. He wasn't the least bit hungry, but what else was there to do? They might as well go have breakfast.

He and Patricia headed down the hall and knocked on the door of the suite. "Y'all come in!"

yelled someone inside. Gregory gave Patricia a quizzical look as he pushed open the door.

"Hey, there, pardner!" A tall man in a white cowboy shirt, blue jeans, and a huge white cowboy hat unfolded himself from a chair and walked over to greet them, a huge, ham-like hand held out for a shake. He grabbed Gregory's hand with an iron grip and pumped it up and down. Then he tipped his hat to Patricia. "Ma'am," he said. "Pleased to meet you. I'm Big Jim."

As if they couldn't figure that out. Who else could it be?

Mom was giving Gregory a look. He knew what it meant. He cleared his throat. "Thank you for letting us stay here," he said.

"And for the plane ride, and everything," Patricia chimed in.

Big Jim waved a hand. "It weren't nothin'," he said. "Least I could do for this dude!" he slapped Steve on the back. "Saved my life, he did! And I'll never forget it."

Steve rocked on his feet. "You've definitely repaid your debt," he said to Big Jim. "We'll never forget *you*, either."

Big Jim chuckled. "I guess you won't," he said. He shot a sympathetic glance toward the couch where Emily lay. "Poor little filly. I sure am sorry about that wild banana boat ride. Bud's an old bronco-busting friend from my rodeo days. Once a cowboy, always a cowboy, I guess."

"I guess," Emily said, with a gracious smile.

Miranda and Lucy jumped up from a big pile of crumpled wrapping paper and ribbons and ran over to hug their cousins. The little girls were subdued, despite the fact that their favorite holiday had finally arrived and they'd been opening presents for an hour already.

Gregory scooped up Lucy and gave her a big squeeze. Poor kid! She'd been looking forward to Christmas for weeks.

"Merry Christmas," Miranda said, looking up at Patricia with sad eyes.

"Don't worry," Patricia said, squatting down to look into Miranda's face. "Cookie will find her way back to us soon."

"That's right," said Big Jim, rubbing his hands. "Now, how about if we all sit down to some grub? We'll talk about how we're going to find those dogs of yours." He pulled the silver dome off one of the plates on the table. "Mmm, I love the way they do home fries here," he said.

They sat down to eat.

"The way I see it, we'll have those dogs home in time for the Christmas parade," Big Jim said as he helped himself to some scrambled eggs. "I've got all my best people out there looking for them, up and down the coast for miles. I even called in a favor from a buddy in the Coast Guard."

"My sand castle–building friend volunteered to

help," Steve said. "Funny, we were so competitive, but now that the castles have washed away, I can't even remember why I cared so much."

"The surfers are going to help, too, I hear," Dad added. "Dakota, and Jinx, and that Mr. J-dog."

"G-Dog," Gregory corrected him. "And Montana, and Jax. Better get it right for your article." He managed a grin. He knew his dad knew the right names. He was only fooling around, trying to get someone—*anyone*—to smile.

"Thomas called last night to say that the environmental club would be out looking today, too," Patricia told everyone. She knew Thomas still felt terrible about his silly act of vandalism. Plus, he really liked Santa Paws. Of course he would want to help.

Everyone wanted to help. Throughout the day, people fanned out all over the island, not just on the beach, but in town, in the restaurants, and at the alligator farm. Jax's cousin came up from the dolphin research facility, and all the girls in Montana's and Gregory's surfing class came out, with their parents.

But the shadows grew long and dusk began to fall, and there was still no sign of Santa Paws and Cookie. Christmas Day was ending, and the dogs had not returned.

Nobody felt much like watching the boat parade, but, as Big Jim had said, "The show must go on!" The Callahans trooped down to the beach.

Steve was holding a sleepy Lucy in his arms. What with Christmas presents and looking for the dogs, she had never gotten a nap that day. Amazingly, she wasn't cranky at all. She just looked sleepy and sad, lying with her head resting on her father's shoulder and her thumb in her mouth.

Mr. and Mrs. Callahan stood holding hands. "Well, so much for Florida," said Mrs. Callahan. "If we had stayed up north, none of this would have happened."

Mr. Callahan hugged his wife close. "Shh," he said. "Don't blame yourself."

"That's right, Mom," Patricia said. "This could have happened anywhere. Santa Paws and Cookie have always put their own safety last."

Gregory nodded. "Remember the time he was rescuing people in that subway fire in Boston?" he asked. "We thought he was a goner then. But he made it!"

"And what about when Cookie braved that blizzard in Maine?" Patricia agreed. "I can just picture her diving through those deep snow drifts."

That made Gregory remember the time Santa Paws had saved his life when he'd had a snowboarding accident. "I wouldn't be here today, if it weren't for Santa Paws!" he said out loud.

"You're not the only one," Dad said. "That dog rescued so many people. He was—he *is* an amazing animal. And so is Cookie. They're both one of a kind."

Everyone was silent for a moment. Then Miranda pointed out to sea. "Look!" she said. "Lights!"

Sure enough, the first boat was just coming into view, leading a chain of vessels lit with so many lights that they looked like a million stars, reflecting in the dark, glossy water. The lead boat was a beautiful wooden yacht—Big Jim's boat. It was ablaze with tiny white lights. The sounds of "Silent Night" drifted over the waves to the shore.

As the boat drew closer, the lights seemed to glow more brightly and the music grew louder.

"Look!" shouted Miranda. "Look!"

There, in the bow, were two of the most beautiful creatures any of the Callahans had ever seen. Their dogs! Santa Paws and Cookie had their paws up on the front railing. They looked toward shore with eager faces: bright eyes, pricked ears, and doggie grins—beneath white fur-trimmed red Santa hats.

Behind them, Big Jim waved a white cowboy hat in the night sky. "Yee-haw!" he said. "Look what I found!"

Patricia began to sob with joy, and Gregory felt his own throat growing tight. Miranda cheered, and Lucy laughed with pleasure. Steve hugged

Emily carefully, so as not to hurt her rib, and Tom Callahan gave Eileen a huge kiss on the cheek. "We may never know where they've been, or what they've been doing," he said. "But I do know one thing. This will make the *perfect* lead for my story!"